The killer liked the press in these small communities. The press focused attention on the killings and rewarded the killer's decision to leave a special message at the scene of each crime. The playing cards had a special significance to the killer that no one would ever understand, but that didn't matter.

The Royal Flush killer was making headlines. Big, bold newspaper copy and lead-off segments on radio and television were making people take notice. Everyone was talking about the crimes, wondering about the cards, devouring the news bites like hungry birds pecking at breadcrumbs.

Soon, the killer would have to move on to other areas. Staying in one place too long was foolish and dangerous, but for now the Royal Flush killer would silently enjoy the attention and the glow of accomplishment that came after the kill.

CAROL COSTA

A DEADLY HAND

WORLDWIDE®

TORONTO • NEW YORK • LONDON
AMSTERDAM • PARIS • SYDNEY • HAMBURG
STOCKHOLM • ATHENS • TOKYO • MILAN
MADRID • WARSAW • BUDAPEST • AUCKLAND

For Frank, my husband and best friend

Recycling programs
for this product may
not exist in your area.

A DEADLY HAND

A Worldwide Mystery/February 2011

First published by Thomas Bouregy & Co., Inc.

ISBN-13: 978-0-373-26740-8

Printed in U.S.A.

Acknowledgments

I would like to thank my agents, Lettie Lee and Andree Abecassis of the Ann Elmo Agency, who are always there to offer services and support.

I am also grateful to the staff of Avalon Books for their expertise and guidance.

Last but not least, I thank my friends from the Society of Southwestern Authors who never fail to encourage and inspire me.

ONE

"'LEONA WAS MURDERED,'" Dana said, repeating the words printed in shaky block letters on the pale blue note paper.

"If it's true, I'll never forgive myself," Sam said.

"Who gave you this?"

"Leona's roommate, a sweet old woman named Helen something or other."

"At the funeral?"

"Yes. I talked to her briefly before the service, and she pressed it into my hand. I didn't think much about it, just stuck it in my pocket. I didn't even read the damn thing until a few minutes ago."

"It can't be true," Dana assured him. "Why would anyone want to murder a lovely old woman like Leona?"

"All I know is Leona called me last Friday. She was very excited, said she had an important story for me. She wanted me to drop everything and come right out to see her." Sam paused and shook his head. "I didn't go, and that same night she died, or was murdered."

"Sam, don't do this to yourself. You're a busy man. Leona has called you dozens of times claiming to have a hot story. As I recall, the last time you went running out there she gave you a tape recording of an interview with the man who reads the gas meters."

Dana felt obligated to make excuses for Sam. Perhaps because her editor seldom showed the kind of emotion she was seeing now. The death of his old friend had obviously left him badly shaken, and now this note had heaped guilt upon his grief.

"I'm going back to Peaceful Pines to talk to Helen," Sam said. "I'd like you to come along. If there's a shred of evidence to support this note, I want you to drop everything and investigate."

"I'll get my coat." Dana stood up and walked over to the chrome rack, where a brown tweed jacket and beige scarf hung. They matched the beige slacks and brown sweater that adorned Dana's trim figure. It was Bruno's favorite outfit. He was expecting her to go to dinner tonight.

"I'm sorry, Dana. I hope I'm not spoiling your plans for this evening. If only I'd read this note earlier." Sam was talking more to himself than to her.

Dana lifted her light brown curls over the collar of her jacket. "It's okay. I want to go with you. I'm sure we can clear up any questions tonight. This Helen is probably just overwrought and confused about Leona's death."

Sam went ahead to get his car, while Dana told her secretary to call Bruno. "Tell him I can't make dinner, but I'll meet him at the Aztec Club about eight-thirty."

Marianne frowned. "He's going to ask me a million questions."

"He can't help it. He's a cop."

"Sam was talking so loud I overheard most of what he said. How much can I tell Bruno?"

"As much as he can wheedle out of you. It'll make him feel better about getting stood up."

Marianne nodded grimly and reached for the phone. Dana hurried outside to meet Sam.

TWO

PEACEFUL PINES RETIREMENT HOME was located in Pine Grove City, about twenty miles from the newspaper office in Crescent Hills, Illinois.

Pine Grove was a quiet, rural community. Many of its residents had relocated there to escape the noise and congestion of Chicago. Others had come because they sought a less stressful, safer environment in which to raise their children.

Well-cared-for homes were scattered on acre lots among the trees that gave the town its name.

In recent years, a few apartment buildings had sprung up and new schools had been built to accommodate the growing population. The commuter train that used to bypass Pine Grove now stopped every morning at six and every evening at five-thirty to load and unload the residents who worked in Crescent Hills and in the downtown area of Chicago.

Older residents feared that the town was growing too much and there was talk of new building codes to stem the tide. Yet, there was still nothing much that actually happened in Pine Grove. By the time the sun set each day, the citizens of the town were all safely home, eating their supper, doing homework, or watching television.

It was after six on this brisk fall evening, and in the business district the stores were closed and dark. Anyone who wanted to shop after six at night drove into Crescent Hills.

The only sign that the town was aware of a world outside its city limits were the reminders of the upcoming statewide elections scattered here and there. Campaign posters were mounted on storefronts and telephone poles. Ordinarily, city ordinances prohibited such displays, but this was a special election. One of Pine Grove City's most prominent residents was running for governor.

Charles Wright's campaign office was sandwiched between the Pine Grove National Bank and the Pine Grove Insurance Agency. His official campaign photograph took up most of the front window. A smiling, handsome face looked out onto the quiet street. Underneath his countenance his campaign slogan warned Don't Go Wrong, Vote for Wright.

In the alley that separated the bank building from the town's one and only grocery store, a derelict was rummaging through the Dumpster. The sky was dark, but the contents of the Dumpster were visible thanks to a single lightbulb hanging over the delivery entrance of the grocery store.

The shabby looking man was not a common sight in Pine Grove. This one had probably wandered into town from the main highway that ran parallel to the railroad tracks.

The middle-aged scavenger muttered to himself as he withdrew a piece of rotted fruit and stuffed it in his pocket.

"Slim pickings," he said, letting his body slide into a reclining position against the sturdy Dumpster. He reached into another pocket of the filthy overcoat he wore and pulled out a pint-sized bottle of wine. He held it up to the light. It was almost empty.

Shrugging his thin shoulders, the man drank from the bottle, draining it in a few swallows. Then, he struggled to his feet and pitched the bottle into the Dumpster.

Turning around, the derelict suddenly realized that he was no longer alone in the alley. A stocky figure dressed in a dark overcoat and a wide-brimmed hat had joined him.

"Hey, buddy," the bum called out. "Can you spare a dollar?"

The newcomer stopped and took a piece of currency out of his overcoat pocket and waved it at the derelict with a black-gloved hand.

Delighted by this gesture, the derelict stumbled forward to meet his benefactor. With his eyes fixed on the currency, he didn't notice that the stranger had taken out another object from another pocket.

The derelict was still concentrating on the currency, intent on making it his. He made only the slightest sound of disbelief as the bullet entered his stomach.

The victim staggered backward, The assailant fired the gun again. This time the derelict was hit in the chest, and crumpled to the ground. The dark figure fired the gun again, leaning over to place the silenced weapon against the bum's temple.

Satisfied that his prey was dead, the shooter stood back and looked down at the stranger who had just been murdered.

Then, the gloved hand reached into a pocket once more, and withdrew the final items. One by one they were dropped onto the lifeless man's body.

Five playing cards from an ordinary deck were now a part of the murder scene. The cards were the Ace, King, Queen, Jack, and Ten of Spades. Together the cards formed the ultimate poker hand, one that most players could only dream of getting: a Royal Flush.

THREE

THE RIDE to Peaceful Pines Retirement Home was filled with long silences broken occasionally by attempts at casual conversation. Dana had a lot of questions she wanted to ask about Leona, but she refrained from asking them. Instead, she tried to remember all the things she'd heard about Leona from Sam and others who worked with the one-time star reporter of *The Globe*.

"Do you think this is a waste of time?" Sam asked, intruding on Dana's thoughts.

"Not if it will put your mind at ease. I was just thinking about the way everyone who worked with Leona talked about her. She must have been dynamite."

"She was. Nothing got by her shrewd little eyes, or escaped that quick wit."

"I'm sorry I never had the chance to work with her."

"You two would have worked well together. You're cut from the same cloth, only a generation or so apart."

Traffic picked up and Sam fell silent again concentrating on the road. His last statement was one Dana had heard before. Sam had often compared Dana to Leona saying that they both had the same desire and ability to dig below the surface of a news story, often uncovering facts that other reporters had missed.

Five years ago, Dana had been a cub reporter who fought off tremors of panic every time the city editor gave her an assignment, but her determination to get the whole story—the true story—had caused her career to move forward at a quick pace.

The Globe was located in Crescent Hills, a growing metropolis close enough to Chicago to be convenient, far enough away not to be considered a suburb of the big city.

Sam McGowan was a man who believed that a daily newspaper should do more than report the news in a community. Two years ago, Sam had created Globe Investigations. Backed by all the resources of the newspaper, its function was to reach out to the community and investigate reports of illegal or criminal activity.

Sam had appointed Dana to head up Globe Investigations. As Crescent Hills grew, so did its crime rate and requests for help came into *The Globe* on a daily basis.

Dana had gone undercover a number of times. Her investigations helped break a string of robberies, uncover a drug ring operating out of the county nursing home, and save an innocent man from prison. In between, there had been the small, less newsworthy cases involving everything from missing persons to fraud at the supermarket.

Currently, Dana had her own office, a secretary, and two other investigative reporters who worked under her supervision. The workload was often heavy but Dana seemed to thrive on it and, like Leona, Dana had become somewhat of a star herself. Her byline was respected and the stories she wrote were hard-hitting and honest.

"How old was Leona?" Dana asked Sam.

"I'm not sure, late seventies, maybe eighty. She's been retired for more than twenty years now."

"Her retirement party was her wedding reception."

"Right, her first marriage at fifty-nine. I guess she never had time for it earlier in life. Anyway, Rosetti was wealthy. Leona took his name and adopted his lifestyle. They traveled all over the world together before he died. I've got a box full of postcards."

"You were more than a friend to her, Sam," Dana said gently. "I only met her a few times when she came to see you, but she was so proud of you. She once told me her favorite cub reporter had grown into a big bear of an editor."

"She got me the job," Sam admitted. "When Jeffers retired, Leona marched into the publisher's office and told him that if he didn't make Sam McGowan editor, he was dumber than she always thought he was."

"You never told me that one before."

"I can hardly believe she's gone." Sam's voice was soft. "Here's the turn-off. I didn't think I'd ever be coming out here again."

Dana glanced at the green-and-white sign on the edge of the highway they were driving on. It said Peaceful Pines Retirement Home 2 Miles. Sam turned off onto a private road.

Dana looked around at the stately pine trees that lined each side of the road. "I understand that Peaceful Pines is quite exclusive."

"By exclusive, you mean expensive," Sam said. "It is, but Leona didn't have to worry about money. Rosetti left her very well-off."

As they got closer, Dana could see the lights of a huge colonial-style building. A brick structure with gleaming white pillars, it was set back from the road and guarded by an army of pine trees and a formidable wrought-iron fence. The lawn in front of the building showed patches of brown from the autumn frosts, but everywhere Dana looked, there was evidence of meticulous care.

"I'll bet this place is filled with flowers in the spring and summer," Dana said.

"It is. Leona said it was the perfect setting for her sunset years." Sam approached the gate and rolled down his window to speak to the security guard.

"Can I help you?" A uniformed man spoke to them from the booth to the left of the gate.

Sam handed him his press card. "I'm here to see

Mr. Templeton. I called earlier to make sure he'd still be here."

The guard nodded and handed the card back to Sam. Then he pushed a button and spoke into an intercom hanging on the wall of the guardhouse.

A few minutes later, the iron gate swung open and Sam guided his car up the winding drive toward the building. They parked the car in the area reserved for visitors and walked up the wide stairs that led to a porch that extended across the width of the building. Various couches and chairs with wrought-iron frames and multicolored cushions were scattered around the porch, but on this chilly fall evening, they were predictably empty.

The door was locked. Sam rang the doorbell and a delightful sequence of chimes announced their arrival. A few seconds later, a young girl opened the door and admitted them.

"Hi. I'm Janet. Mr. Templeton is in his office. I'll show you the way."

The inside of the building was as impressive as the outside. The coldness of white marble was softened and warmed by soothing blue and green tones in the plush carpeting and heavy draperies.

Dana noted that the upcoming elections were an important event at Peaceful Pines. The lobby was filled with campaign posters and literature. They seemed like an obtrusive reminder of the chaotic world that existed outside the walls of this stately retreat.

As Dana passed one of the tables, she picked up a flyer that invited the residents to meet the candidates at a special rally. The rally had taken place the previous week, several days before Leona's death. Dana folded the flyer in half and slipped it into her purse.

Janet turned left at the end of the lobby, and Dana and Sam followed her down a corridor that seemed to contain only the offices of the staff. She stopped in front of an open door and motioned them inside.

John Templeton stood up and greeted them with a smile that was too big for his pinched, oblong face. Dana's first impression was that if the tall, bony Mr. Templeton walked into *The Globe* dressed as he was tonight, he would be taken directly to the obituary desk.

"Mr. McGowan, I was surprised to hear that you were coming back tonight. I'm sorry, but I'm afraid Mrs. Rosetti's things are not together yet."

Sam waved off his apology. "This is one of my reporters, Dana Sloan. Sit down, I want to talk to you." Sam's voice and manner were curt, as if the very sight of Templeton aroused his anger.

Templeton politely shook Dana's hand and remained standing until his visitors settled into the upholstered chairs facing his desk.

"Is something wrong, Mr. McGowan?" Templeton was suddenly nervous.

"I don't know. That's what I'm here to ask you."

"Oh..." Templeton rose again and walked behind

them to close the door to his office. "This way we won't be disturbed." He sat down again and looked expectantly at Sam. "How can I help you?"

"I'd like to speak to Leona's roommate, Helen. I don't know her last name. We spoke briefly at the service this morning and..." Sam stopped as he noticed the strange look that had come over Templeton.

"Is there something wrong, Mr. Templeton?" Dana asked.

"Yes, as a matter of fact, I'm afraid something very unfortunate has happened. Mrs. Johnson, Helen, was taken to the hospital just a few hours ago. She's suffered a stroke. We're afraid the stress of losing Leona may have triggered it. They were very close, you know."

"Yes, I know," Sam said slowly. "That's why it's so important that I speak to her."

"I'm sorry. She's not allowed any visitors at this time, and frankly, the prognosis isn't good."

"I'll be damned," Sam said. "First Leona, now Helen—what in the blazes is going on here?"

"I beg your pardon?" Beads of perspiration began to form on Templeton's brow. He produced a neat white handkerchief and dabbed at his forehead.

"Sam," Dana intervened. "Perhaps if we just explain why we came out here this evening, Mr. Templeton can clear it all up for us."

"Yes, please," Templeton agreed. "I'll help in any way I can."

Sam reached into his pocket and handed Templeton

the note. Templeton's hands were shaking as he unfolded it, and when he read it, the remaining color drained from his face.

"Helen Johnson gave me that at the funeral," Sam explained. "Unfortunately, I didn't read it until I was getting ready to leave the paper this evening."

Dana and Sam stared at John Templeton waiting for him to say something to reassure them that Leona's death was a natural occurrence.

Instead, Templeton looked back at them with panic in his eyes. "I was hoping to keep this quiet."

"What?" Sam was on his feet, and Dana had to move quickly to step between her editor and the director of Peaceful Pines. Sam looked as if he might snap Templeton's scrawny neck.

"Please, don't be angry," Templeton pleaded. "I'll explain as best I can."

Dana and Sam took their seats again. Dana rested her hand on Sam's arm in a sign of support. "Then there is some question about Leona's death?" she asked as diplomatically as possible.

"Yes, I'm afraid there is," Templeton admitted.

"Start at the beginning," Sam ordered in a menacing tone. "And don't leave out any details."

Templeton nodded and wiped his forehead again. "Leona's body was discovered early Saturday morning by one of our nurses, Mrs. Morrison. The body was immediately removed from the room and brought to our infirmary, until it was picked up by the coroner's men."

"What about Helen? Had she called for help? Sounded an alarm?" Sam asked.

"No, she did not. When Mrs. Morrison entered the room, it was on the routine morning wake-up call. Although Helen was very upset, she gave no indication of anything else. We also have a security man who patrols the building at night. He didn't see or hear anything out of the ordinary. We didn't think Leona's death was anything but a natural passing."

"And what changed your mind?" Sam leaned forward in his chair again.

"Whenever a resident dies unattended here, the procedure is to have an autopsy performed by the county coroner. Please believe me. Nothing like this has ever happened at Peaceful Pines before. Our security is top-notch. Our staff is carefully screened."

"Get on with it," Sam demanded.

"The autopsy showed that Leona was smothered to death. Particles on her skin indicated that she was suffocated with a pillow, yet Mrs. Morrison insists that Leona's bed was undisturbed. She was found lying on her back, with the pillows placed properly beneath her head."

"Have the police been here?" Dana asked quietly.

"Of course. A Sergeant Milecki from the Pine Grove Police Department was here. He took all of Leona's personal belongings. He also questioned some of the staff and Helen."

"And what did Helen tell the police?" Sam asked.

"Nothing. She said she was asleep and didn't know

anything about Leona's death. And no one except myself and the authorities know about the autopsy report. The people questioned were told it was simply a formality because Leona died unattended."

"Then why did Helen give me that note?" McGowan stood up again. Dana didn't try to stop him.

"I wish I could answer that question," Templeton replied. "Perhaps after she thought about it, she remembered something."

"Maybe Helen was too frightened to say anything to you or the police," Dana suggested.

"I was really hoping to avoid any bad publicity," Templeton continued. "Peaceful Pines has a reputation for giving the very best care to our residents."

"At the very highest prices," Sam added cynically.

"Please, Mr. McGowan, I understand how upset you are over this. I am equally disturbed to have such an unthinkable thing happen here."

"So what are the police going to do about this?" Sam asked.

"Not very much, I'm afraid. I don't know if you're aware of this, but we've had a series of bizarre murders in this area. Milecki told me straight out that the police are more concerned with that than the questionable death of an eighty-year-old woman."

"Are you referring to the Royal Flush murders?" Dana asked.

"Yes, of course. I forgot you're news people. Naturally, you'd be aware of what's going on in your surrounding communities."

"Two of the murders occurred in Crescent Hills," Sam told him in an impatient tone. "But I expect our police department to treat all homicides with equal priority."

Templeton nodded, agreeing with Sam without commenting on the editor's critical view of Pine Grove City's investigative techniques.

Dana turned to her editor. "Sam, I think our next step is to talk to the police. It's obvious Mr. Templeton doesn't know much more than we do."

Sam nodded and now Templeton stood up quickly. "Look, I hope I can count on you to keep all of this confidential. As I said before—"

"No, you can't count on it," Sam bellowed. "A very dear friend of mine has been murdered, and I'm going to holler like hell until I find out who did it. And if that means using all the resources of *The Globe,* so be it."

Templeton blinked and swallowed, and Dana felt genuinely sorry for the man. "Please, I assure you that I will do everything I can to find out who violated our serenity here. I intend to call in a private investigating firm first thing in the morning."

"That won't be necessary," Dana told him. "I'm an investigator for *The Globe.* I'll be handling this case personally."

"Oh, I didn't know," Templeton stammered.

"Dana heads up Globe Investigations," Sam said.

"She and her staff look into many unexplained and dubious situations. Dana is especially good at digging below the surface and getting to the truth."

Templeton nodded. "I see."

"I could go undercover here," Dana said thoughtfully. "Surely you have an unimportant position you could slip me into."

"Well, I suppose..." Templeton was clearly overwhelmed by the idea.

"If the murderer is someone on your staff, he or she could strike again," Sam said coldly. "Maybe they already have. Helen's stroke could have been induced by unnatural methods."

"Oh, God, no!" Templeton fell back into his chair, his thin face suddenly bathed in sweat.

"If you allow me to work from the inside, we can guarantee you a quiet investigation. Otherwise..." Dana let her voice trail off and shook her head causing her curls to bounce around her face vigorously.

Before Templeton could answer, his intercom buzzed. "The hospital is calling on line two," a young voice announced into the office. "It's about Helen Johnson."

Templeton reached for the phone. Sam and Dana waited while he spoke to Helen's doctor. "Helen is stabilized," Templeton told them as he hung up the telephone.

"How soon can she have visitors?" Sam asked.

"Not for a few days. Even then, I'm not sure if she'll be of any help. According to the doctor I just spoke to, Helen is partially paralyzed and at this time is unable to speak."

"Damn it!" Sam slammed a hand on Templeton's desk.

"How about that quiet investigation, Mr. Templeton?" Dana's hazel eyes were cool, and her pretty face held a stern expression. Her mind was already calculating the first steps of her inquiry into Leona's death.

"Let me think about where I could slip you in," Templeton said. "An evening shift would probably be best. Of course, I will have to clear it with our board of directors."

"Here's my card." Dana offered him a plain white card from her purse. "Call me at my office tomorrow morning."

Templeton nodded. "Thank you. I will." He walked around his desk and opened the door for them.

Sam had fallen silent. Dana took his arm and guided him out of the office. Then, as if it were an afterthought, she turned back to Templeton. "Do you have a list of Leona's things? The police usually make one up."

"I believe so."

"May I see it, please?"

Templeton hurried back to his desk and removed a sheet of paper from the center drawer. "I'll make a copy for you."

A small, sleek machine in the corner of his office quietly slid out a copy of the list, which Templeton handed to Dana.

"Thank you. I'll talk to you tomorrow, then."

Templeton nodded again, then quickly closed the door of his office behind Sam and Dana.

"I think Templeton would rather sweep this mess under his plush carpeting," Dana told Sam as they walked to the car.

"He was awfully nervous. I think he knows more than he's telling."

"Possibly. I'll have Bruno check with the Pine Grove police and get whatever information they've gathered."

"Pretty convenient having a homicide detective for a steady boyfriend, huh?" Sam's teasing remark was the first hint of humor he had displayed that night.

FOUR

SAM AND DANA RETURNED to *The Globe*. They stopped in the coffee shop in the lobby of the building and picked up sandwiches and coffee and carried them upstairs to Dana's office.

Sam called his wife to tell her he'd be home in an hour or so. Dana unwrapped her sandwich and thought if she hadn't had to cancel her dinner date with Bruno, she could have been enjoying a thick, juicy steak instead of dining on cold tuna fish. She also wondered how upset Bruno was going to be when she finally showed up at the Aztec Club.

As an investigative reporter, having a detective for a boyfriend did have its advantages. It could also be pretty exasperating. Detective Al Bruno was like a team of runaway horses. Sometimes, Dana felt like she would choke on all the dust their relationship kicked up.

Bruno's old-fashioned Italian upbringing had implanted certain beliefs in him. He thought a woman should stay at home cooking pasta and nursing babies. Dana was not currently interested in either prospect, but no matter how often she made that clear to Bruno, he continued in his quest to tie her down. Underneath the warmth and affection of their relationship was that constant challenge to meld their individual beliefs into a long-term truce. Maybe that was what kept them together.

Sam finished his phone conversation and sat down to eat his sandwich. "If that creep Templeton doesn't cooperate, I'm going to plaster his bony face all over the front page."

"You really dislike him. Why?" Dana asked as she took a small sip of the hot, strong coffee.

"Just a gut reaction, I guess. Where's that list you got from him?"

"In my purse, it was too dark to read in the car." Dana snapped open her bag and produced the sheet of paper Templeton had given her. She began to read it to Sam. "Toothbrush, assorted toiletries and cosmetics, gold locket, wedding ring, dominoes, bible, dictionary, thesaurus…"

"Still the star reporter holding on to the tools of her trade," Sam commented.

"Wait a minute." Dana looked up and down the list, and then handed it to Sam.

Sam studied the list for a moment then laid it down on Dana's desk. "Her tape recorder and tapes aren't listed," Sam said slowly. He got up and paced back and forth in front of Dana.

"That hot story she called you about. She had it on tape, of course."

"I don't know. My God, Dana, do you think Leona

could have really stumbled onto something important?"

"What did she tell you about the story?"

"Nothing really. It was one of those hectic days, and I wasn't paying close attention. Mainly she just wanted me to drop everything and come right out to see her." Sam hesitated and closed his eyes as if his failure to rush right out to Peaceful Pines made him an accessory to Leona's murder.

"All right," Dana said firmly. "Let's not jump to conclusions. Leona's story may have been nothing at all."

"Or it could have been so important she was murdered to keep it quiet." Sam let out a sigh of frustration and crushed the paper around his half-eaten sandwich. "If only I'd gone out there when she called me, if only..." He stopped talking and reached for his coat. "I've got to get home. Emily is waiting for me."

Dana understood what Sam was really saying. He wanted to be alone with his guilt.

Silently, they left *The Globe* building. Sam walked Dana to her car and waited while she got inside and started the engine.

"Be careful driving home," Dana said softly. He nodded and turned away. "Sam?" He turned around to face her again. "It wasn't your fault. You know that, don't you?"

"Yes. I know, but it doesn't help much."

"I'll find out who did it."

"That would help."

Sam walked into the darkness toward his own car, his shoulders slumped, his steps slow and deliberate.

"I'll find out for you, Sam," Dana said again. She guided her car out of the parking lot, hoping she was making a promise she would be able to keep.

FIVE

THE APARTMENT WAS DARK, but the Royal Flush killer liked it that way. The night was a friend, a cloak that hid many imperfections that glared forth in the sunlight.

The secondhand furniture with its sagging cushions and scratched surfaces didn't look so shabby when the lights were off. The same was true of the kitchen appliances that were chipped and gray with age.

The killer could have afforded a nicer apartment, better furniture and new appliances, but had long ago learned to live simply, meagerly.

Expensive possessions were unnecessary when life itself had so little meaning.

The long oversized coat and hat were carefully stored away in the back of the bedroom closet. The sleek black gun with its fancy silencer was hidden away with the gloves and the knife with the long razor-sharp blade.

Tonight the gun had been the weapon of choice, although killing with the knife was definitely more satisfying. Stabbing a victim was more personal and sometimes resulted in the pleasure of seeing the victim's life force escape slowly. A gunshot was sometimes so instantaneous the victim was dead before hitting the ground. Of course, the result was the same—the elimination was completed. Alternating weapons was simply a device to complicate the police investigations.

The other garments worn that night were dropped into the laundry basket on the floor of the closet. The killer now stood naked and satisfied, breathing in the stillness of the night.

The stuffy, cramped bedroom housed only a small dresser and a single bed. The killer moved to the bed. Clean sheets and a warm blanket welcomed a body weary from walking the cold streets in search of a victim.

In the morning, a long hot shower would once again wash away the feeling of accomplishment and joy that came after each murder, but tonight the feeling clung like an expensive silk robe, smooth and soothing.

Pine Grove City was the last place the killer had expected to make a kill, yet the opportunities had continued to present themselves. The community was growing, spreading closer to more urban areas and therefore attracting more of the soiled, gritty street people. The derelicts obviously didn't read the local paper, weren't aware of the others that had been eliminated in the area.

Even if they were aware of the danger, perhaps the lure of the affluent community and the upscale offerings of its trash containers were too great a temptation.

The killer smiled and thought about the most recent victim. When was the last time the man had slept in a bed or enjoyed a hot meal?

Was there a family who wondered where he was or why he had abandoned them to live in the streets? Was there anyone on the face of the earth who would care that he had died tonight?

The police would be troubled by the crime. The residents would be shocked and puzzled by another murder in an area once untouched by violence. For Sale signs would begin to appear in front of the lovely houses. Children would be watched more carefully, protected more diligently by frightened parents. That was another positive result of the killings, but good people, especially children, had nothing to fear from this killer.

It was only the lowest level of society that had to be afraid. The filth needed to be swept away, the smell of liquor and the stain of garbage buried deep in the earth where it could no longer touch decent, hard-working people.

The mission to rid society of the bottom feeders, the festering sores of humanity, had begun long ago. In the big cities, many of the deaths had garnered little attention from the authorities.

Even in death, the bums were ignored. With so many murders occurring on a regular basis, big-city cops tended to work only those cases that involved victims that mattered. Citizens that contributed to society were important, their murders were reported by the press and investigated by the police. The bums were a scourge, an embarrassment to the cities where they dwelled in alleys and begged on street corners. They were not missed. Morgues overrun with unidentified corpses disposed of them quickly and efficiently, just as the killer had done.

After a while, it got to be unfulfilling. Why keep on with the mission if no one noticed or cared? Moving into the smaller, more affluent communities made victims harder to find, but the satisfaction factor had soared. Murders were not a daily or even monthly occurrence in the upscale areas. Therefore, any killing was investigated and reported by the press.

The killer liked the press in these small communities. The press focused attention on the killings and rewarded the killer's decision to leave a special message at the scene of each crime. The playing cards had a special significance to the killer that no one would ever understand, but that didn't matter.

The Royal Flush killer was making headlines. Big, bold newspaper copy and lead-off segments on radio and television were making people take notice. Everyone was talking about the crimes, wondering about the cards, devouring the news bites like hungry birds pecking at breadcrumbs.

Soon the killer would have to move on to other areas. Staying in one place too long was foolish and dangerous, but for now the Royal Flush killer would silently enjoy the attention and the glow of accomplishment that came after each kill.

SIX

THE AZTEC CLUB WAS LOCATED a few blocks from *The Globe* in the downtown area of Crescent Hills. It was a small, quiet tavern that appealed to an assortment of reporters, off-duty cops, and court employees.

Bruno was waiting for her in their usual corner booth. Leaning back, casually sipping a beer, his shirtsleeves rolled up and his tie pulled loose, Bruno looked more like a football player than a detective. He stood up to help Dana with her jacket and flashed the brilliant smile that made his dark eyes crinkle at the corners.

"I ordered you a gin and tonic," Bruno said. "I figured you could use it after such a long day." Dana slipped into the booth across from him. She took a long, slow sip of her drink, and smiled gratefully. "Did you have dinner?" Bruno asked.

"Sam bought me a tuna fish sandwich. How about you?"

"I'll order a pizza." Bruno went up to the bar to place his order. Dana took another sip of her drink and gazed at the television set that was behind the bar.

With the state elections a few weeks away, the

airwaves were filled with political commercials. The handsome blond features of Charles Wright, the leading gubernatorial candidate graced the small screen. Under scenes of Wright shaking hands and working in his law office, his campaign slogan flashed across the screen.

"Don't go wrong, vote for Wright." Bruno repeated the slogan in a singsong voice as he came back to the booth. "I might be tempted to vote for that guy if it wasn't for that stupid slogan."

"You're supposed to make a decision based on the issues and the candidate's abilities. I think Wright would be a good governor. I like his youth and enthusiasm." Dana nodded in agreement with her own words.

"Go on. You just like him because he's good-looking."

"Another point in his favor," Dana teased.

"He's just another rich guy trying to buy his way into a political office."

"Okay, Bruno," Dana said patiently. "I'm sorry I had to cancel our dinner date."

"Who said anything about that?"

"You're trying to pick an argument."

"Yeah." He grinned. "Then we can kiss and make up."

Dana leaned across the table and kissed him lightly on the mouth. "I really am sorry."

She reached for a handful of his thick black curls, but Bruno backed away too quickly. He shrugged his broad shoulders and took a drink of beer. "What about the old girl Marianne told me about? Did someone really murder her?"

"Yes, and I need you to call the Pine Grove City police and get some information for me."

"That's the only reason you go out with me, isn't it? I'm what you reporters call a source."

Dana laughed. "You're a source, all right—of what I'm not exactly sure. So will you call Pine Grove for me, please? A Sergeant Milecki is handling the case."

"A good man. We're meeting tomorrow to exchange information on the Royal Flush cases."

"That is such a bizarre case. Casey wants to do a special story on it."

Bruno sat up straight and glared at Dana. "Look, sweets, tell your skinny assistant to butt out. We've got enough trouble with the public on our necks every minute to find this lunatic. You reporters tramping all over the crime scenes and rehashing every detail only makes it worse."

"She's not going to interfere with your investigation."

"Sure. You always say that, then the next thing I know she's calling me up, asking for favors. Well, you girls want favors, call the party supply store."

Dana picked up her drink and drained the glass. She set it down quietly and smiled at Bruno. "I know what you're doing, Bruno. You're trying to get me angry so I'll tell you not to bother helping me with the Rosetti case. Well, it's not going to work. Call me tomorrow, when you have some information."

Dana was out of the booth and heading for the door before Bruno's bulk could restrain her. Outside, she pulled on her jacket and hurried toward her car. She was almost there when Bruno caught up to her. As he tried to grab her, Dana swung her purse at him. For a big man, Bruno had excellent reflexes. He ducked and managed to get Dana trapped in his arms in one swift move.

"I'm warning you, mister," Dana said trying not to laugh. "I know judo."

"So do I," Bruno replied. "Little Chinese guy works out of the twelfth precinct in Chicago."

Bruno's kiss was always surprising to Dana, passionate, yet full of gentle affection. This was one part of their relationship that didn't need work. Passing cars honked at them as they stood on the sidewalk kissing. Finally Bruno released her.

"You'd better get that pizza to go," Dana suggested.

An hour or so later, they were eating cold pizza in Bruno's bed.

"I really do love you, lady," Bruno said.

"I know you do. That's why I put up with your awful disposition."

"Go on. You've been conning me since the day we met." Bruno continued his speech in a falsetto. "Oh, Detective Bruno, I just need one tiny bit of information, and I'll be ever so grateful to get it."

"And don't I always remember to say thank you?" Dana licked pizza sauce off her finger.

Bruno grinned and winked. "Yeah. Sometimes more than once." He leaned back against the pillows and closed his eyes.

"Did I tell you about the missing tape recorder?" Dana asked.

Bruno opened one eye. "The old reporter's?"

"Right. I want you to ask the Pine Grove police about it."

Bruno groaned and sank deeper into his pillows. "All the nice women in this world, and I have to get involved with a lady gang buster."

"Sam thinks Leona may have uncovered a hot story and that's why she was murdered."

"Get serious, honey. What kind of a hot story could an eighty-year-old woman living in a retirement home come up with?"

"I picked up an old flyer over there tonight. There was a political rally at Peaceful Pines the week before Leona's death. Your favorite gubernatorial candidate was there."

"As much as I dislike his slogan, I don't think he's the type who murders old ladies. What about the age-old motive of money. Who profited from Leona's death?"

"A small college in Wisconsin. She left everything to their Journalism Department to be used for scholarships."

"Great, just what this country needs, more reporters."

"I'll ignore that remark, because you just said you loved me and because you are going to help me with this case."

Bruno groaned again as Dana jumped on top of him. "Please, Detective Bruno," she teased in a high voice. "I'll be ever so grateful."

SEVEN

SOMETIME DURING THE NIGHT, Bruno was called out to a murder scene and wasn't there when Dana woke up. He left her a note saying they would try for a proper dinner date again that evening.

She drove home to shower and change for work and arrived at *The Globe* a little before nine.

The morning sky was dark with clouds and Dana had decided to defy the gloom by wearing one of her favorite outfits. Her suit was a bright shade of blue. It had a pleated skirt and a loose-fitting jacket that hung over a red blouse with a high ruffled neckline. Her shoes and purse were also red.

Despite the problems she was trying to sort out concerning the Rosetti case, Dana was feeling pretty sprightly. Funny how a night in Bruno's arms made her feel so special and loved, while the prospect of making it a permanent thing scared the hell out of her.

Various people greeted Dana as she rode the elevator up to the twelfth floor of the building where her office was located.

Marianne was talking on the phone when Dana entered the reception area. Her secretary was a natural redhead with a lovely heart-shaped face. People, especially male people, often referred to Marianne as a "knockout." Fortunately, Marianne's office skills were as excellent as her looks.

"No, I'm sorry," Marianne was saying into the phone. "Miss Sloan hasn't come in yet, can I take a message?" Marianne listened and her green eyes began to flash with merriment. "No way, buster, I'm not going to tell her that."

Dana looked at Marianne quizzically as she passed in front of her to enter her private office. Marianne mouthed the word "Bruno."

Dana nodded as Marianne resumed her conversation. "Hold on, she just walked in. I'll transfer you."

Pulling off her coat and tossing it over a chair with one hand, Dana picked up the phone with the other.

Dana's office was nicely decorated with dark wood furnishings. An L-shaped desk was placed in front of a large window that overlooked the downtown area. There were several chairs and a few small tables between the desk and a large credenza against the opposite wall. A color television occupied the center of the credenza and was flanked on each side by healthy green plants and family photos in matching silver frames.

File folders and reports were neatly stacked on the desk around the computer and telephone console, indicating that the workload was heavy, but the worker was organized and efficient. The front page of *The Globe*'s morning edition was already spread across the center of the desk. The headline read Killer Deals a Deadly Hand.

Dana glanced at it as she spoke into the phone. "Hi. What's going on?"

In his office across the street from *The Globe,* Detective Al Bruno's desk looked like a hurricane had passed over it. Stacks of papers, fast food sacks, and stained coffee mugs obscured the surface of the desk and overflowed onto an adjacent chair and the floor.

Bruno's size-12 feet rested on top of the cluttered desk. He leaned back in a high-backed chair large enough to comfortably contain a man of his size. He was tired and in need of a shave, but that didn't cut down on the number of smiles and waves he got from the females who passed by his desk.

"I watched the sunrise over the latest victim of the Royal Flush killer," he told Dana. "Found him in an alley in Pine Grove City."

"Did you find any new clues?" Dana asked.

"No, but forensics is still working on the scene."

"Maybe they'll turn up something significant."

"Right. I'm going home to shower and catch a nap. Just wanted to make sure we were still on for tonight."

"I'm looking forward to it."

"Good. I'll pick you up at seven. And do me a favor, don't wear that blue suit with the red blouse. It makes you look like you just stepped out of a phone booth."

Obviously Bruno had seen Dana as she entered the building downstairs. While Dana loved the brightness of the suit and the red accessories, Bruno always said it reminded him of Superman's getup.

"Go to hell, Bruno," Dana said calmly as she dropped the phone into the receiver with a clunk.

Dana hung up her coat and sat down behind her desk. Marianne came in with a cup of coffee and handed Dana a few messages.

"Bruno's in a good mood this morning," Marianne observed.

"He got called out to a murder scene in the middle of the night. It makes him slaphappy."

Marianne shuddered. "Those killings are so gruesome. Poor Bruno, you'd better be extra nice to him tonight."

Dana flipped her hand through her unruly light brown curls, still slightly damp from their morning shampooing. "Sounds like he's been coaching you again."

Marianne laughed. "You should hear what he wanted me to say."

"Something about cooking his pasta and having his babies?"

"Something like that. There's an article about Mrs. Rosetti on the obit page. Did you know her?"

"Not well," Dana replied. "But I have a feeling I'm

going to get to know her very well before this case is resolved."

Laughter erupted from the reception area and Dana knew that her investigators, Bob Farrell and Casey Jordan, had arrived for their weekly meeting.

Soon everyone was gathered in Dana's office going over the current cases they were working and discussing their next assignments.

Bob was a very plump young man with a jovial look while Casey was just the opposite, thin and serious.

As they talked, Bob munched on a candy bar. "Tell me something, Dana," he said with a serious expression on his cherub face. "Why did you assign this diet center thing to me?"

Dana suppressed a smile. Bob was setting her up, and she loved it. "Well, Bob, it was a tough decision, but then the scales just seemed to tip in your direction."

Bob nodded as if he was taking this answer to heart. Marianne and Casey were both smiling, knowing that something else was coming.

Bob didn't disappoint them. "Speaking of scales, they make me weigh in every day. They've got one of those electronic scales that talks."

"I've read about those," Marianne told him.

"Yeah, well anyway, every time I get on this scale it says, 'Come back when you're alone.'"

The women all laughed while Bob shrugged and took another bite of his candy bar.

"Now seriously, Bob," Dana said. "What do you have to report?"

"I think the complaints we got were unfounded. The place seems on the level to me."

"Not if that candy bar is part of your personal weight loss program," Casey remarked.

"Absolutely not," Bob said. "This is part of another cause that is near and dear to me: Save the whale."

The girls laughed again, then Dana sobered and called for order. "Enough, Bob. Give it another week, and then turn in your final report." She turned to her female investigator. "Casey, you did a great job nailing down the city hall rumors. Even Sam was impressed."

"Thanks," Casey murmured. "With the elections coming up so soon, it wasn't easy to get information."

Marianne grimaced. "The guy I was going to vote for withdrew from the race because of our investigation. I have rotten taste in men."

"That's because you judge men on the basis of their looks," Bob told her. "I keep telling you, a good looking wrapper doesn't mean a thing. It's what's inside that counts." To demonstrate, Bob held up his empty candy bar wrapper and crushed it.

"Oh, go talk to your scale," Marianne said.

Casey interrupted the verbal contest. "Dana, I wanted to ask you if you talked to Sam about my looking into the Royal Flush murders. One of the victims was an old man who hung around my mother's neighborhood."

Dana recalled the words she had exchanged with Bruno the night before on this very subject. "I'm not sure we should get involved in a police case of this magnitude," she replied carefully.

"I know," Casey insisted. "I didn't mean that I wanted to investigate the murders. I was thinking more of doing something on the street people and how their danger has made people more aware of their plight."

Sorry, Bruno, Dana thought to herself. Aloud she said, "You're right, Casey. It would make a good feature. Go for it, but it will have to take a back seat to your regular assignments."

The rest of the staff meeting dealt with new investigations that needed to be started. Dana assigned everything to Bob and Casey. She, herself, would be spending all her time and energy on the Rosetti case.

With this in mind, Dana left her office and rode the elevator down to the second floor, where *The Globe*'s political department was buzzing with activity. Dana made her way through the maze of desks to a glass-enclosed office.

Bernie Singleton was the paper's top political columnist. At the moment, his fingers were flying across the computer keyboard. Dana waited until he stopped and acknowledged her presence.

"Hi, pretty lady," he said, smiling as if he were glad for the interruption.

"Hi, Bernie. Looks like you're buried here."

"Never too busy to talk to you. What's up?"

Dana got right to the point. "I need background information on some of our illustrious candidates." She handed Bernie the flyer from Peaceful Pines, and he studied it for a few seconds.

"All but one of these guys have been around for years. Why? Because they keep their noses clean and don't make waves. In other words, they are boring as hell."

Dana nodded at his assessment of the State's current slate of candidates. "Okay," she said. "So tell me about Charles Wright."

Dana sat on the edge of his desk while Bernie leaned back in his chair and gazed up at her. "A bright new star on the political horizon. He's well educated, a successful lawyer, an impressive speaker, and good-looking and rich enough to wage a spectacular campaign. I say he's going to the Governor's Mansion."

"No skeletons lurking in his closets?"

"Not one discernible rattle. In fact, the one flaw in him is that he's so perfect. It makes one suspicious."

Dana laughed. "Come on, Bernie, don't make me beg. What's the inside scoop on Mr. All-American? And what about Mrs. All-American? Other than a few fuzzy photographs, she's been nonexistent during this campaign."

"Health problems." Bernie opened his desk drawer and removed a photograph, which he handed to Dana.

It was the type of black-and-white photograph used by actresses and models. Dana's hazel eyes opened wide as she viewed the young woman in this particular photo. She was very beautiful, and dressed in a revealing outfit, looked very buxom and sexy. The name at the bottom of the photo said Madeline McKay.

"She looks pretty darn healthy to me," Dana told her fellow reporter.

"It's an old photo. Seems Mrs. Wright once did some modeling and pursued an acting career. In recent years, she's been suffering from a chronic back condition that keeps her close to home and off the campaign trail."

"So far you haven't told me anything I couldn't have read for myself in the candidate's press releases."

Bernie resumed an upright position behind his desk. "Look, Dana, there's no real scoop here, only unconfirmed gossip." Dana stared at him levelly, waiting for him to continue. "Okay. Rumor has it the lady is kept under wraps because the marriage is on the rocks."

"Why is the marriage on the rocks?"

"Who knows? Look, I'll tell you the same thing I told Leona. If you can find out, you tell me."

Dana's trim figure jolted off the desk. She grabbed Bernie's arm. "Hold it. Leona Rosetti asked you about Charles Wright?"

Placing his hand over Dana's, Bernie smiled and nodded. "That's right. The old gal was still on the job. She met Wright and like any good reporter realized he was too good to be true."

"When did you talk to her?" Dana asked.

"Last week, I think. I'm not sure what day it was. We're so busy around here, they all seem to run together."

Dana slipped her hand from Bernie's grasp and began to back out of the office. "My cue to leave. Thanks, Bernie. You've been a big help."

"Hey, wait a minute. Aren't you going to explain what's going on?" Bernie shouted. "If you've got dirt on Wright, I want in on it."

"I'll keep you posted," Dana promised.

When Dana got back to her office, she called John Templeton, and asked him about the political rally that had been held at Peaceful Pines.

"Leona was interested in Charles Wright," Dana told him. "Do you know if she had a personal interview with him or any contact with him after the rally?"

"I'm sure she did not," Templeton replied. "After the speeches, the candidates left for another engagement. I suppose Mrs. Rosetti could have called him, but residents are not allowed to leave the home without an escort and our records indicate she did not arrange for any type of outing."

"Okay," Dana said. Not satisfied with his answer, she decided to drop the issue for the moment and moved on to the other reason she had called him. "Have you made arrangements for me to become a staff member there?"

"Well, I've been thinking that a nighttime position would work best. Perhaps you could take over Janet's duties at the reception desk."

"Fine. I can start tomorrow evening. What time?"

"Tomorrow?" Templeton repeated. "I don't know..."

Dana cut him off midsentence. "The sooner I start, the sooner this situation can be resolved."

"Oh, yes. Of course, you're right. Can you be here by four?"

"Absolutely," Dana replied firmly. "I'll see you then."

With that settled, Dana sorted through the morning mail. Requests for *The Globe*'s investigative staff were mainly received by mail. The majority of letters contained trivial complaints that could be handled with a return letter or a simple phone call. Sometimes a reader wanted help with a serious problem like a missing person, or some type of fraud. Some letters provided information on a crime. Thankfully, today's mail didn't contain anything that required immediate attention.

Dana's intercom buzzed. Marianne said Sam McGowan was on line one.

"Hi, Sam."

"Did you hear back from Templeton?"

"I just spoke with him. I'll be working in the reception office of Peaceful Pines in the evenings. I start tomorrow."

"Maybe it won't be necessary," Sam told her. "I just checked with the hospital and we can visit Helen Johnson this afternoon."

"Are you saying she can talk to us?"

"She still can't speak, but I'm hoping we can find some way to communicate with her. I think she holds the key to Leona's death."

"I hope so," Dana said sincerely.

EIGHT

SAM AND DANA WAITED outside the Intensive Care Unit at Crescent Hills Memorial Hospital, where Helen Johnson was a patient.

A young Hispanic nurse dressed in white slacks and a smock adorned with colorful butterflies came out of Helen's room and motioned them inside.

"You can only stay ten minutes," the nurse cautioned as they slipped past her.

Helen was hooked up to a variety of monitors. Her snow-white hair was frizzed around her pale face. Her eyes were closed, but her breathing was shallow enough to indicate that she was not actually asleep.

Sam and Dana moved to either side of Helen's bed. Sam placed his hand gently on her shoulder and the old woman's eyes fluttered open. She looked at Sam and recognition flooded her face. She tried to speak, but could only make a noise that sounded like a deep sigh.

"Helen," Sam said quietly. "This is Dana Sloan. She's an investigative reporter who is helping me look into Leona's death. I'm very sorry I didn't read your note sooner, before you were taken ill."

The old lady stared up at Sam. Her faded blue eyes slowly filled with tears.

"You don't have to be afraid, Helen," Sam reassured her. "You're safe here." He paused and let that message register, then continued. "I know you can't speak, but I'm going to ask you some questions. If the answer is no, do nothing. If the answer is yes, close your eyes and then open them again. Can you do that?"

In reply, Helen closed her eyes and opened them again. Sam and Dana both smiled in relief.

"Do you know who hurt Leona?" Sam asked.

Helen's eyes remained open, but she seemed to be straining to remember something.

"Did you see anyone in your room the night Leona died?"

Helen's eyes closed and then opened again.

Sam and Dana looked at each other. "Did you see John Templeton that night?" Sam asked.

Helen's eyes remained open.

"Someone else on the staff?" Dana added.

Helen's eyes remained open, but once again she seemed to be straining to remember something.

They didn't have a suspect list and couldn't ask Helen about anyone else specific, so Sam tried another approach.

"Do you know why someone would want to hurt Leona?"

The blue eyes opened and closed.

"Did it have something to do with a story she was working on?"

Again, Helen closed and opened her eyes.

"Do you know what the story was about?

Helen's eyes filled with fear again, and tears began to slide down her withered white cheeks. Dana took a tissue from a box on a bedside table and gently wiped them away.

The Hispanic nurse came back into the room. "You're upsetting my patient," she scolded. "You will have to leave."

Sam turned on his most charming smile. "Please, it's very important that we ask her a few more questions."

The nurse was not swayed. "I'm sorry. In her condition, a few minutes are as tiring as a few hours. She pushed the call button, which probably spent the last of her energy for today."

Sam and Dana looked back at Helen and saw that she had closed her eyes again.

"What now?" Sam asked as he and Dana drove back to *The Globe.*

"Drop me at my car," Dana instructed. "I'm going to drive back to Pine Grove City."

"I thought you weren't starting at the retirement home until tomorrow."

"I'm not. In the meantime, I want to try and speak to Charles Wright or someone on his staff. His campaign headquarters are there."

"What does he have to do with this?" Sam's voice was strained.

"Probably nothing," Dana replied casually. "But he was at the political rally held at Peaceful Pines, which means Leona may have talked to him. He's the most high-profile candidate."

"The one who could be destroyed by a hot story," Sam noted.

"It's a long shot," Dana assured him quickly. "I just want to cover all the bases."

Dana didn't feel she should share the information Bernie had given her about Leona's phone call to him. A political figure's reputation could be trashed with one ugly rumor and she didn't want to jeopardize Charles Wright's campaign without substantial proof of wrongdoing.

NINE

CHARLES WRIGHT'S CAMPAIGN office was a bustling place. Volunteers stuffed envelopes, answered phones and greeted visitors.

Dana introduced herself and showed her press card to the woman who was seated at the desk closest to the door. "I called a half hour ago and was told I could have a few moments with Mr. Wright."

"Oh, yes," the elderly woman agreed. "Mr. Wright is always happy to talk to the press. Please have a seat, and I'll see if he's off the telephone."

The woman got up and walked to a closed door just behind the desk. Dana watched as the volunteer knocked briefly and then, not waiting for an answer, swung the door open.

Seated behind a desk that seemed too small for his large body, Charles Wright was even better looking in person, but apparently he had been in the midst of an unpleasant phone conversation.

"Call me back in an hour, and I'll give you an answer," he said curtly, slamming the phone back into its receiver. Ignoring the volunteer who had come into the office, Charles Wright yelled past her. "Paulette, come in here."

Undaunted by the candidate's irate manner, the volunteer stepped forward. "Miss Sloan from *The Globe* is here to see you."

Instantly, Charles Wright erased the angry look from his face. "I need a few minutes with Paulette. Please ask Miss Sloan to wait."

Dana continued to stand at the receptionist's desk. By this time, Paulette had been summoned from the back room by one of the other volunteers. Paulette was a tall, slim woman with short black hair. Dana classified her as attractive rather than pretty. Her sleek look and stature were further enhanced by her clothes. A pale green business suit that probably cost as much as Dana made in a week was accessorized with black patent leather pumps and ebony jewelry.

Paulette rushed past Dana into Wright's private office. The volunteer, who reminded Dana of her own grandmother, came out as soon as Paulette went in, but due to her advanced age wasn't able to close the door fast enough to keep Dana from overhearing the first few words spoken between the candidate and his assistant.

"Someone got to Madeline," Wright said tersely.

"How?"

"He didn't say."

Then the door closed completely, cutting off the sound of their voices. The volunteer smiled at Dana, seemingly unaware of any problem.

"Mr. Wright will be with you shortly. Would you like some coffee?"

"No, thanks," Dana replied, returning her smile.

Dana settled into a chair that looked like it had been taken from a fancy hotel lobby. While she waited for Charles Wright and Paulette to finish their emergency meeting, she mentally reviewed the conversation she'd had that morning with *The Globe*'s top political columnist.

Bernie said that the official word on Madeline was that she wasn't able to campaign with her husband because of a chronic back problem. The unofficial scoop was that the marriage was on the rocks. Maybe, Dana mused, because there's hanky-panky going on between Charles and his assistant, Paulette.

Dana based her latest assumption on the look Paulette had on her face when she breezed past Dana. Paulette's face was shining with anticipation as if she couldn't wait to step into the presence of Charles Wright.

There had been no hint of annoyance or impatience at having been called away from whatever she had been working on. A campaign manager's job was very hectic. Interruptions were expected, but usually not welcome. Yet Paulette's expression indicated to Dana that this campaign manager was delighted by the interruption and unexpected summons to Wright's office.

Dana turned her thoughts back to the few sentences she had managed to overhear before the door closed and cut off the rest of Wright's conversation with Paulette.

"Someone got to Madeline." Words spoken in a voice filled with emotion meant only one thing to Dana—Madeline Wright knew things that the candidate didn't want known. But the bigger revelation was the last thing Dana heard.

Wright said, "*He* didn't say."

So the caller was a man, a man who had talked to Madeline Wright, or gotten information from someone else who had talked to Madeline Wright.

Wright's office door opened again, interrupting Dana's thoughts. Paulette walked out and extended a beautifully manicured hand to Dana.

"Thank you for waiting, Miss Sloan," she said sweetly. "I'm Paulette Mason, Mr. Wright's assistant. He'll see you now."

Dana shook her hand. "Nice to meet you."

Without further pleasantries, Paulette escorted Dana into the candidate's office. Wright was standing in front of his desk with a smile so broad he looked like he was posing for one of his campaign photos.

Paulette backed out of the office, closing the door behind her as Dana and the handsome candidate shook hands. His hand was warm and smooth, his handshake as impressive as his looks.

"Please have a seat," Wright said, steering Dana toward a chair much like the one in the reception area.

Dana sat down and adjusted her skirt.

"I'm delighted to meet you," Wright continued

as he slid into the high-backed black leather chair behind his desk. “I’m actually a big fan of yours.”

“Thank you,” Dana replied. “But you don’t have to flatter me. I’ve already decided to vote for you.”

Wright rewarded her with another dazzling smile and a warm chuckle. “I appreciate that. Now what can I do for you today? I know you don’t write political features, so I hope you’re not here to investigate me.”

“No, I’m not.”

He smiled again, and nodded for her to continue.

“On one of your campaign stops, you visited Peaceful Pines Retirement Home.”

“Yes, a lovely place filled with lovely seniors.”

“A friend of mine met you that day. Her name is Leona Rosetti. Do you remember her?”

Wright frowned. “I don’t think so. Is there some reason I should?”

“She’s a retired newspaper reporter. Sometimes she still does stories for *The Globe* and I’m sure she would have approached you for a personal interview.”

Dana was making it up as she went along, and hoped it sounded plausible.

“Oh, of course,” Wright agreed. “The sweet old lady with the tape recorder. I’m sorry, I didn’t remember her name.”

“Then you did give her an interview?”

“Well, not right then. We were on a tight schedule

that day. I gave her my card and told her to call and we would arrange a time for me to come back out and talk to her again."

"And did she call you?" Dana asked.

"No. At least I don't think she did. Why?"

"Mrs. Rosetti was murdered."

Dana's intention was to catch the candidate off guard and observe his reaction.

"I'm so sorry," Wright said, quickly. "I didn't know." His voice sounded sincere, and his body had sprung to attention. Either her announcement had truly startled him, or he was a terrific actor. "What can I do to help?" he added.

"Could you check with your staff, both here and at your home, and see if any of them remember talking to Mrs. Rosetti?"

"I can check with the office staff, but she didn't have my home phone number," Wright said. A slight twinge of mistrust edged his voice. "And it's unlisted."

"I'm sure it is," Dana told him firmly. "But the murdered woman was a reporter, adept at searching out information not available to the general public."

Wright suddenly seemed to realize that any lack of cooperation would cause Dana to view him in a different light. He smiled at her. "Of course. I'll be happy to have Paulette talk to our servants and report back to you."

"What about your wife?" Dana asked. "Could she have spoken to Mrs. Rosetti?"

Now Wright became visibly uncomfortable. Dana assumed it was because he had connected her last question to the phone call he had received.

"Not likely," he replied carefully. "My wife is not well and does not take phone calls or see visitors."

He's lying through his beautifully capped teeth, Dana thought.

She stood up, and Wright politely rose to his feet. "I won't take any more of your time," Dana said. Taking a business card from her jacket pocket, she offered it to him. "Please call me if anyone remembers speaking to my friend."

"Certainly. Do you have any suspects?"

"Not at the moment." Dana let the statement hang in the air as she turned and left the office.

Paulette was hovering outside the door, waiting to talk to Wright the moment Dana left.

As Dana walked to her car, she smiled to herself. Thanks to her, the candidate and his personal assistant would have a lot to talk about.

TEN

"WHAT DID SHE WANT?" Paulette asked, seating herself in the chair that Dana had just vacated.

"She's investigating a murder, a retired reporter from her newspaper who lived at Peaceful Pines. I actually remember the old woman—she had a tape recorder and asked me for a private interview."

"And?"

"I probably told her to call you to arrange it." Charles stopped and stared into space as an angry flush colored his handsome face. He stood up quickly and walked to the front of the desk. "Good God, Paulette. Do you think she's the one who got to Madeline?"

"The old lady from the retirement home?"

"Yes."

"How the hell should I know? You'll have to ask your wife."

"It's beginning to make sense. Madeline was in town when I made the rounds of the senior citizens groups. I even tried to get her to accompany me. The old folks like to see the wife and kiddies."

Paulette quickly put words to the scenario Charles was working on. "The old lady interviewed Madeline.

Madeline said some nasty, unflattering things and then somehow, the tape fell into the hands of this guy who is trying to blackmail you."

"That's what I'm thinking."

"The next logical conclusion is that the guy may have killed the old lady to get the tape."

Charles ran a hand across his worried face. "I told him to call back in an hour." He glanced at the inexpensive watch on his wrist. It was a poor substitute for the Rolex that Paulette thought too flashy for the campaign trail. "We've got thirty-five minutes to decide what to do."

ELEVEN

AT FOUR-THIRTY the following afternoon, Dana was walking down the hall of Peaceful Pines with John Templeton. The first floor branched off from the lobby into three different sections. Staff offices, dining room and kitchen, and rooms for female residents.

Their first stop was the dining room where workers were preparing the tables for the evening meal.

White linen, gleaming silverware, crystal glasses and pale blue china plates adorned each table. Crystal bud vases with a single flower were being positioned in the center of each round table. Despite the lighting that was bright and plentiful, it looked like the dining room of an upscale hotel.

There was an elevator in the dining room and Templeton ushered Dana inside and pushed the button for the second floor. They passed through the recreation section where Dana peered into the various rooms. The main lounge held a movie screen, a refreshment bar and rows of straight-backed chrome chairs arranged theater-style. The television room contained the largest set Dana had ever seen. An afternoon talk show was on, but no one was in there to watch it.

There was also a craft room with long tables and supplies stacked on them. Posters and photos of recent projects hung on the walls of the room.

The library walls were lined with bookshelves and volumes of hardcover books, but no one occupied the chairs or sofas scattered about the room.

"Most of the residents are in their rooms at this time of day," Templeton explained. "They like to rest or freshen up before the evening meal."

However, when they looked into the billiards room, there were four old gentlemen arguing over whether one of them could make the shot on the table.

"You'll sink the eight ball, and they'll win," one of them complained.

"Will not," his partner replied. "I could make this shot with my eyes closed."

"Stop jabbering and do it then," a man from the opposing side suggested.

In addition to the recreation rooms, the male residents were housed on the second floor. Dana followed Templeton down another hallway with rooms on either side of it.

The doors to some of the rooms were standing open and Dana could see that they were nicely decorated with color-coordinated linens and draperies. Each seemed to have a private bath and most were furnished with easy chairs and assorted tables and lamps. They looked clean and comfortable.

At the end of this corridor there was an atrium with lots of green flowering plants. Across from the atrium was a glass-enclosed office where a tall, willowy woman dressed in white was seated behind a metal desk sorting through a stack of papers.

"Mrs. Hatterly, I'd like you to meet Dana Summers. She'll be taking Janet's place in the reception office for a few weeks. Dana, this is Margaret Hatterly."

Dana smiled and extended her hand. Mrs. Hatterly shook Dana's hand, but did not return her smile.

"Margaret is the supervisor for this shift. She's in charge of the gentlemen residents who occupy this floor."

"I assume it's pretty quiet here in the evenings," Dana said as an attempt at friendly conversation.

"There are many activities for the residents," Hatterly replied. "Obviously you're not familiar with this type of facility."

"No, I'm not," Dana agreed in the same friendly tone. "I hope I can count on you for help when I need it."

The woman remained stern. "You'll be working on the first floor, so I suggest you count on Mrs. Schmidt to help you. Since I stopped working the day shift, I rarely leave the second floor."

Templeton nervously tried to smooth things over. "Mrs. Hatterly just transferred to the three-to-eleven shift last week," he explained hastily.

Back in the elevator, Dana questioned Templeton. "What reason did Mrs. Hatterly give for changing shifts?" The woman's unfriendly demeanor had aroused Dana's suspicions.

"She said it was for personal reasons. Since she has seniority, I complied with her request. I make it a point not to be too inquisitive."

"So I've noticed," Dana told him, covering the insult with a sweet smile. Templeton didn't bother to answer.

The elevator deposited them back on the main floor and Templeton led her around a corner past the rooms occupied by the female residents of Peaceful Pines. All of the ladies' doors were closed, but Dana assumed their rooms were pretty much the same as the ones she had viewed upstairs.

"This place is like a huge maze," Dana said. "Do you provide maps to new employees and residents?"

"You'll find a copy of the layout of both floors attached to the wall in the reception area."

They approached another glass-enclosed nurses' office. Through the glass, Dana saw another white-clad figure sitting behind another desk. This office and its furnishings were identical to the one upstairs: metal desk, generic desk chair, beige file cabinets across one wall, and two straight-back chairs for visitors.

Mrs. Schmidt was an attractive blond woman with an ample figure and bright blue eyes. She looked up and caught sight of Dana and Templeton and hurried to the door to greet them. Dana estimated her age to be around forty, about the same age as Hatterly.

"Good afternoon, Mr. Templeton." The nurse spoke with a slight European accent. Probably German, Dana surmised.

Templeton introduced Dana. This time when Dana smiled and extended her hand it was grasped warmly.

"Please, call me Erna," the nurse said. "And I will call you Dana, such a lovely name."

"Thank you," Dana replied. "It's nice to meet you. Mr. Templeton tells me that you are the evening supervisor."

"Yes, and Mrs. Hatterly is also a supervisor, upstairs on the men's floor."

Dana nodded. "Yes. I met her."

Their attention was then diverted by a man also dressed in a white uniform who entered the office carrying a stack of clean linens. As he lowered his burden to the top of the desk, he looked at Dana and winked.

"Hi. I'm Peter Hogan." He reached out and shook Dana's hand. He was a few inches shorter than his boss, but where Templeton was thin to the point of looking frail, Hogan was broad and muscular. His hair was the color of light caramels, neatly cut and styled. He had nice brown eyes and a nicely trimmed beard. "I couldn't pass by without finding out who the new lady was."

"Dana Summers," Dana replied, letting the made-up last name slip easily from her lips. "I'll be working in the reception office for a few weeks."

"Great. Then we'll be seeing a lot of each other. And I'm betting you'll be a big hit with the old gentlemen."

"Peter," Templeton said pointedly. "Don't let us keep you from your work."

The young man nodded without comment, picked up the linens again and hurried on his way.

"Peter is the one to call if you have any problems at the desk," Erna said after he left. "Or if he's not around, you call me."

"Thank you," Dana was really grateful for the offers of help. Although the job sounded simple enough, she had never worked as a receptionist and felt there was more to it than Templeton would admit.

There didn't seem to be many residents around at this time of day. As they walked back to Dana's post in the reception office, again Templeton explained that was because it was close to dinnertime.

"They have their big meal at noon, and then a light supper at five. Most of the residents are in bed by nine at the latest."

"I see," Dana said.

"Someone from the kitchen staff will bring you a tray," Templeton continued. "You can eat at your desk."

Having already shown her around the small reception office, Templeton said he had a church meeting and had to leave right away. Dana was rather glad to see him go. Something about the man made her uneasy.

Alone in her new office, Dana sat down behind the desk and stared at the telephone console. It was just like the ones they used at the newspaper, except this one had a built-in intercom so she could page people who didn't answer their phones.

She got up and walked around the office. A long worktable was set up in the back with a few folding chairs stacked against the wall. The floor plan Templeton had mentioned was attached to the wall behind the table and chairs. The edges of it curled around the tacks that held it in place. Dana surmised that it had been there for several years.

A lone file cabinet stood against the third wall. It was locked. Dana thumped the side of it. It sounded empty. An artificial plant with dusty leaves and yellow flowers sat on top of it.

A small door behind the file cabinet in the corner of the room opened into a miniscule bathroom. There was a commode and a tiny sink. An oval mirror with a floral frame hung over the sink. Dana peered into the glass and patted her hair. Her natural curls had a mind of their own. When she needed a haircut as she did now, they sprung out in various directions, wispy coils of soft brown flecked with gold.

A buzzing sound made Dana sprint for the desk and the telephone console. "Good afternoon, Peaceful Pines," Dana said a little breathlessly.

The call was for someone named Marco, who worked in the kitchen. Dana transferred the call without a problem, and sat down at her desk and began looking through the drawers. Nothing unusual there: stationery, envelopes, pens, pencils, paper clips, and a supply of phone message pads like the ones stacked on the desk. Little packets of sugar, salt, and pepper were strewn in the bottom of one of the drawers. In place of a computer, there was an aging electric typewriter. Dana turned it on. It worked.

A counter and a sliding glass window separated Dana from the lobby.

"Well," she mused softly, "all I need now is for the murderer to walk up to this window and confess."

TWELVE

DANA WAS JUST PICKING UP her fork when she received an ominous warning.

"Don't touch that, unless you have a death wish."

Dana looked up, her fork poised in midair. An elderly man leaned through the box-office-type window in front of Dana's desk.

"Pardon me," Dana said. Her visitor had a round face with an impish grin, and bright blue eyes. "Can I help you?"

"Nope. I'm trying to help you." He smiled and nodded smugly. His full head of hair was white and wavy. Dana thought he looked like Santa Claus without a beard.

"Why don't you eat at home, before you come here," he suggested. "That way, you won't get acidita."

"What's that?" Dana put her fork down and looked longingly at the meal that had just been brought to her from the kitchen. It looked pretty good to her.

"You know, like on television with the Alka Seltzer."

Dana laughed. "Indigestion?"

"That's right. So what's your name, pretty lady?"

"Dana." She extended her hand to the merry-faced gentleman.

"Rocco Colosimo. My friends call me Rocky," he said as he squeezed her hand. "I like your name. It's like a song, but your hands are cold as ice. Better drink some coffee. It's safe tonight. I saw them scrub the coffee pot today."

Dana removed her hand from his grasp and took a sip of her coffee. She was starving, but she didn't want to hurt Rocky's feelings by ignoring his warning.

"You know, Rocky, I didn't get any lunch today. Do you think I could just chance a few bites of the meatloaf?"

Rocky made a face and shook his head. "No meat-loaf, they scrape up all the leftovers from last week to make that. Stick to the peas and ensalada."

"Thanks." Dana picked up her fork again and scooped up some peas. They were a little bland, but tasted good. The salad was cold and crisp with a mild French dressing.

Rocky stood patiently watching her eat. "So what happened to Daisy Mae? She get mad and quit?"

"I'm not sure who you're talking about," Dana said. "If you mean the girl who usually works here at night..."

"Yeah, that's who I mean. Her name is Janet, but I call her Daisy Mae, because she dresses like the cartoon lady. You dress nice, and you are better looking too."

"Thank you. I'm just filling in for Janet while she takes a vacation."

"And I know why she needed a vacation. I told that Miss Snooty Snoot that Daisy Mae didn't like her using this office for her monkey business, but she doesn't listen to me. When she comes down here tonight, you tell her to get lost."

Dana had no idea what Rocky was talking about, but she smiled and nodded. Templeton had warned her before he left this evening that it was always important to deal tactfully with the residents.

"What does this lady do that annoys Janet so much?" Dana asked.

"Just lock the office door, and don't let anybody in," Rocky said firmly. "I have to go now."

Dana watched Rocky move slowly toward the corridor that led to the recreation room. A list of the week's scheduled activities was posted above her desk. Dana glanced at it and saw that it was bingo night.

The telephone console buzzed and Dana answered it with the required greeting.

"This is the vice-squad," the caller said in a menacing tone. "We've had a report that a bingo game is in progress there."

"Bruno, I told you not to call me here," Dana whispered into the phone. She looked around, checking to see if anyone else was in the lobby. It was empty. "And how did you know it was bingo night?"

"What else can those old folks do to amuse themselves?"

The console buzzed again. "Hold on," Dana instructed. The call was for another member of the staff and Dana used the paging function of the phone console to pass the call on.

Dana returned to the line Bruno was on. "Did you get anything from the Pine Grove police?" she asked quietly.

"They haven't even run Leona's things through the lab. I'm going out with Milecki. They just found another Royal Flush victim a few minutes ago."

"Don't forget to ask him about the tape recorder. Templeton claims he personally gathered Leona's belongings for safekeeping, and those items were not in her room."

"Sure, Dana," Bruno said in a patronizing tone. "Getting you information is my top priority. We can chat about your case while we look over the murder scene. After all, what's a string of brutal serial murders compared to the case you're working on."

"Thank you, darling," Dana said pleasantly as she hung up on him.

Dana was still thinking about Bruno's sarcasm when a tall, large-boned woman entered the office carrying a black bag. Her silver gray hair was pulled away from her angular, yet soft-looking face and secured into a neat twist at the back of her neck.

"Can I help you?" Dana asked pleasantly.

"No, thank you, dear. I'll just set up in the usual place."

The woman moved to the back of the office and placed the black bag on the top of the table. Then, she opened it up and began to remove its contents, laying them in a neat row on the table. There was a stethoscope, a thermometer, blood pressure gauge, tongue depressors, and a small flashlight. The last thing out of the bag was a white lab coat, which the woman slipped her long arms into and buttoned over her plain navy blue dress. Then the woman selected a folding chair and set it up in front of the table.

Dana knew she should probably say something to the woman, at least find out what she was intending to do there in the office, but she was so fascinated by the woman's air of confidence that Dana just stood and watched her. Then, she remembered her conversation with Rocky. Could this be Miss Snooty Snoot?

"There we are," the woman announced when her tasks were completed. "Just send them in one at a time, please."

"Are we expecting visitors?" Dana asked, walking to the back of the office to confront her guest. It was then that the old woman seemed to see Dana for the first time.

"Oh...who are you?" She pulled down the rimless glasses she wore and squinted at Dana. "Where's Janet?"

"She's on vacation for a few weeks. I'm Dana. I'm taking her place. And you are?"

"Dr. Powers, Dr. Mary Powers."

"How do you do," Dana said, offering her hand.

"Fit as a fiddle," Dr. Powers replied. Then, looking over Dana's head, she called out. "Come right in, Louise. I'm all ready for you."

Dana turned to see the office door was now open and another elderly lady entered. This one was as round as she was tall, wearing a red polka dot dress that made her look even wider.

"Just a minute," Dana said walking toward the mass of red dots.

"I'm next," a voice called out from behind Louise. "Mrs. Sobitsky…tell Dr. Powers. Mrs. Sobitsky is next." Dana looked past Louise and the fat woman darted past her with amazing agility and plopped into the chair Dr. Powers held out for her.

"Can I get in next?" another voice, this time a male one, shouted from the doorway. "I want to play bingo too."

Dana couldn't believe her eyes. In a few short minutes, a line of elderly people had formed in the lobby. Dana went to the door, and the old people all stared at her. "Who are you?" Several of them voiced the question at the same time.

"I'm Dana, the new receptionist. Can one of you explain to me what's going on here?"

"Sure." A red-faced little man stepped sideways

out of line to speak to Dana. "We're waiting to see Dr. Powers. Can I be next? I want to play bingo too."

"I'm next," Mrs. Sobitsky told him in a loud voice. "If you want to play bingo, you shouldn't come on Wednesdays. Come back tomorrow."

"I'm a sick man," he said rubbing a wrinkled hand across his ruddy cheeks. "I have a fever."

"Oh..." Dana was about to run to the phone to call a nurse for him, when Peter Hogan showed up.

Dana called out to him. "Peter, can you help me, please?"

Peter cut through the line of residents and presented himself to Dana. "I suppose Templeton ran off and left you to fend for yourself." He grinned at her.

"Well..." Dana stammered a little. "He said he had an important meeting. He also said Wednesday nights were very quiet and..." Dana looked back at Dr. Powers. She was now taking the fat lady's blood pressure and clucking her tongue disapprovingly.

"Too much salt, Louise. It's up again," Dr. Powers said sternly.

Dana turned back to Hogan. "This man here says he has a fever. Maybe you can take care of him."

"Dr. Mary will handle it," Peter said with a wink. "Can you believe it? Eighty-five and she's got more energy than I do."

"Can you explain what is going on here?" Dana pleaded.

"Don't worry," Peter assured her. "It happens every

night—every weeknight, that is. Dr. Mary doesn't see patients on weekends." Peter motioned for Dana to follow him into the lobby, and, wanting to hear the rest of his explanation, she complied.

"Is she really a doctor?" Dana asked when they had moved out of earshot of the residents, who were waiting in line.

"She sure is. Worked at some big hospital in Chicago until they made her retire."

"How long has she been doing this?" Dana jerked her head in the direction of the office.

"Ever since she moved in here, about two years now. The other residents love the attention, and she loves giving it to them. Templeton thinks it's good for all of them, and Dr. Mary's office hours are very short."

"I see, but what if one of them is really sick? I heard a woman had a stroke here a few days ago." With Dana's mind relieved about Dr. Powers and her patients, Dana decided to seize the opportunity to ask Hogan a few other questions.

"You must mean Helen. Yeah, a real sweet old girl. We think she was overwrought about the death of her roommate. Did you hear about that?"

"No," Dana lied. "What happened?"

"Nobody really knows." Peter dropped his voice into a more confidential tone. "It's all hush-hush, but the cops were here investigating. They questioned some of the staff."

"Really? Did they question you?"

"Yeah, no big deal."

"So why were the police here?" Dana persisted.

"They think someone may have murdered the old girl. She was smothered with a pillow, at least that's what the coroner's report said."

"How did you know that?" Dana asked. "I mean, if it's supposed to be so hush-hush."

"Nothing in this place is confidential for long. The old folks tell everything they overhear. None of them can keep a secret. And the staff, well you know how fast a rumor mill can spread a story."

A female voice came over the PA system interrupting their conversation.

"Peter Hogan, report to the nurse's office."

Dana recognized the accent as belonging to Erna Schmidt.

"Whoa, that's Erna looking for me. Gotta run." Peter winked at her again. "I'll see you later."

Pete sprinted down the corridor and Dana went back to her office and watched Dr. Powers examine her patients. As Peter said, the doctor's office hours were short. She saw about a dozen patients, giving each one about five minutes of her time before shooting them out with instructions for a happier, healthier life. "Not too many sweets, watch that salt intake. Take a walk around the grounds tomorrow. Relax and think about the fun times in your life."

Dana answered a few phone calls and exchanged pleasantries with the residents as they filed in and out.

"Thank you, my dear," Dr. Powers said as she

packed up her black bag and removed the white coat. "You were a big help."

"I don't think so," Dana replied. "But I'll do better tomorrow night." *At least I'll be prepared,* she thought to herself.

The rest of the evening passed quickly. Dana met the activities director as she hurried out after the bingo game that had been held in the dining room. She was an energetic and attractive brunette in her mid-thirties. She promised to fill Dana in on weekly activities the next time she saw her.

As it neared bedtime for the residents, Dana watched Erna handle her ladies. She had a firm but gentle way of guiding them along. Her affection for the residents was apparent, and they responded to her suggestions without any complaints.

By nine o'clock, the halls of Peaceful Pines were dark and quiet. Dana met four more staff members who stopped and introduced themselves as they left the building. They were all teenagers who worked part-time. Apparently getting some of the residents settled down for the night took some doing.

"Our job is to give them some extra attention," one of the girls told Dana. "Leave the light on, get me some water."

"What's for breakfast tomorrow?" another girl added.

Dana quickly ruled out all four as suspects in Leona's death. They were high school kids who put in their hours here to earn spending money. She would be surprised if the police had bothered to question any of them.

Earlier Dana had also ruled out the people who worked in the kitchen and dining room. That area was cleaned, locked down, and deserted by 7:00 p.m.

Of course it was possible that one of the teenagers or one of the kitchen staff had gotten back into the building in the middle of the night and killed Leona, but it was highly unlikely. Murders were committed by people who had motive and opportunity. Dana could not fathom that anyone from either group would have had one or the other.

Dana closed the office for the night. Incoming phone calls would now be answered by Erna from her office.

Dana had learned that Erna, Peter, Mrs. Hatterly, and another orderly that Dana had not met, remained on duty until eleven, when a very sparse night shift took over.

The night shift consisted of one nurse and two night watchmen. One guard stayed at the front gate and the other patrolled the halls inside. Dana definitely wanted to talk to all three of them about the night Leona died.

Tomorrow she would get information on them from Templeton. It would enable her to start conversations with each of them and maybe uncover new information about Leona's death.

THIRTEEN

"THIS IS NOT THE WAY I want to spend my only day off," Bruno complained.

Dana patted his arm. "I know, and I really appreciate your going with me."

"Just remember that later," he grumbled. "This guy has got to be a weirdo. Having a press shindig on a Sunday afternoon when the games are on."

"As I recall," Dana told him patiently, "Charles Wright played football in college. I'm sure he's still a fan of the game. In fact, I'll bet he'll have a television set on hand so you can socialize and watch the game at the same time. Just don't get so caught up in it that you forget why I brought you along."

Bruno leered at her. "You mean it wasn't for my good looks and charm?"

"As devastating as they are, today I'm more interested in your powers of observation."

"Don't you think Wright is going to be on guard when he sees you brought a cop to his party? A few days ago, you questioned him about a murder and today you show up at his door with me. How did you get yourself invited to this thing anyway?"

"Bernie gave me the invitation."

"So he could stay home and watch the Bears game."

Dana laughed. "Probably. Anyway, the invitation said I could bring a guest. You're my boyfriend, so bringing you as a guest is perfectly logical."

"But you're not a political reporter."

"I am a reporter," Dana insisted. "And I work for a very prestigious newspaper."

"How come you're zoning in on Charles Wright? I can't see what he might have to do with the case you're working on."

"Leona talked to Wright at a rally at Peaceful Pines. He admitted that she asked him for an interview."

"Sounds like you're grasping at straws."

"Thanks to you."

"Look, sweets, I've already told you that Milecki doesn't want to share information on an open homicide case with a reporter."

"You didn't even ask him," Dana replied. "Admit it."

"I didn't ask him," Bruno said. "And if you're going to give me a hard time about it, I'll drop you off at Wright's door and go home and watch the Bears game."

Dana leaned over and kissed him on the cheek. "No hard feelings."

"Damn."

Dana fell silent. Bruno was right. She was grasping at straws. She was going to this political function hoping to find a new lead to follow.

So far, working at Peaceful Pines had not uncovered any useful information. She had sent Bob to interview the nurse and guards who were working the midnight shift the night Leona was murdered. She couldn't do it herself without revealing that the new nighttime receptionist was actually an investigative reporter.

Bob's interviews had added up to a big fat zero. The nurse claimed one of the second floor residents had a stomachache and she had spent all night ministering to him. The outside guard said no one came or went through the front gate after midnight. He had, however, admitted that it was possible for a staff member to gain access to the building in a number of ways that would bypass his post.

The inside man claimed that he made rounds through the building every hour on the half hour and had not seen or heard anything or anyone on that night.

Bruno pulled his dark green Mercury Cougar into the Wrights' circular driveway. Uniformed attendants were waiting to park the guests' cars. One of them opened the passenger-side door and helped Dana alight. She waited on the porch, thinking that the outside of Wright's mansion looked a lot like the building that housed Peaceful Pines Retirement Home. White pillars and white trim gleamed against the red brick constructions of the two-story colonial-style house.

Bruno relinquished his car to the attendant and

escorted Dana to the front door that was immediately opened by a butler clad in dark slacks and a white coat.

"Just like the movies," Bruno muttered. "Any second Scarlett O'Hara will be sweeping down that staircase, or some kid will slide down the banister."

Dana ignored him and presented their invitation. The butler barely glanced at it before directing them toward a doorway to the left of the foyer.

As they moved toward it, Dana took notice of the elegant marble-floored entrance surrounding the wide staircase carpeted in tones of brown and beige. The walls were painted a pale shade of blue and adorned with a number of beautiful landscapes. Dana urged Bruno toward one of the paintings to get a closer look.

"This is lovely," she said, gazing up at the wooded scene filled with brilliantly colored wild flowers.

Although she didn't have much time to devote to it, Dana loved to paint. She specialized in oils and landscapes, so she was especially appreciative of others who captured the beauty of nature that she tried to project onto her own canvasses.

"Miss Sloan," Charles Wright's deep, warm voice greeted her from a short distance behind her. "How nice of you to come."

Dana pulled her eyes away from the painting and took the hand that Wright held out. "I'm covering for my friend, Bernie. He couldn't make it today."

"I know Bernie has season tickets to the Bears' games. Nice of you to fill in for him." He smiled and extended his hand to Bruno. Dana introduced them. "You look like a football fan," Wright said after he and Bruno exchanged greetings and handshakes. "There's a big screen television in the library, just to the right of the ballroom."

"Good thinking," Bruno replied.

"Please, go on in and enjoy the refreshments," Wright said as another set of guests appeared at the front door.

Dana and Bruno walked across the foyer and down three steps into the room where dozens of people were already gathered.

It was an immense room. One wall was constructed of glass from floor to ceiling, broken in the middle by French doors that opened onto a patio with a low brick wall. Beyond the patio was a garden. A few brightly colored leaves still clung to the trees and the last remnants of fall blooms could be seen here and there, struggling against the chill wind that blew on this overcast October day.

Bruno left her to get drinks from the bar that was built into the back wall. Behind the bar were mirrored walls and shelves crammed with bottles and glasses. Dana smiled and waved at the people she knew from other newspapers and the radio and television stations, but didn't want to waste time with party talk. She was here to observe, to get a feeling for Wright's home ground and see if she could garner any information about the mysterious Madeline.

The conversation she had overheard between Wright and Paulette had continued to nag at her. "Someone got to Madeline."

Although Dana knew it was a long shot, she couldn't shake the thought that the someone who got to Madeline was Leona Rosetti.

Against the third wall across from the patio doors the center of a buffet table as long as a football field held a huge ice sculpture of a waterfall that ended in a pool of blue water with floating gardenias.

White-clad waiters stood behind the table at various positions serving the guests from what seemed to be an endless variety of food.

Scattered around the room were small round tables draped in white linen where the guests could eat and talk and drink. All in all, the reception was a spectacular demonstration of the candidate's wealth and his desire to make a good impression on the press people who could influence their readers and help Charles Wright become the next governor of Illinois.

The candidate had returned to the room and he was working the crowd, moving skillfully around the room, smiling and chatting with his guests. Dana glanced at the podium set up just to the right of the entranceway. Once the guests were all fed and plied with booze, Wright would make a speech and answer questions.

Dana began to scan the room looking for Paulette.

She spotted Wright's attractive assistant near the buffet table. She was dressed in a white pants suit and lots of gold jewelry. The blazing lights on the chandeliers danced across her glistening black hair. Interesting, Dana thought, touching the short curls that remained after her quick trip to the beauty shop yesterday. That's definitely a dye job, so dark the light can't penetrate one strand. I wonder who her hairdresser is?

Bruno returned with a beer for himself and a glass of white wine for Dana. "Are you hungry?" he asked.

"I can wait," Dana replied. "Go check on your football game. And while you're in the library, see if you can find a trace of Wright's wife in evidence. Maybe a photo or something."

"I thought the lady dressed in white with the jet-black hair was his wife. She's glad-handing everyone."

"Mrs. Wright is a buxom redhead. That woman is the candidate's campaign manager slash personal assistant. Her name is Paulette Mason. Maybe you should run a background check on her."

"I'm sure you've already done that."

Dana smiled. "Yes, but I didn't uncover anything sinister, or even very interesting."

Bruno gave her his patronizing smile. "Tell you what, Nancy Drew. Try to get her prints on a wine glass and then we can run them through the FBI computer."

"That's not a bad idea. Come on, I want you to meet her."

"After I check on the game," Bruno said.

"On your way to check on the game," Dana told him.

She took Bruno's arm and together they maneuvered their way over to Paulette's station at the buffet table. It was near the open door that probably led to the library and the television set, so Bruno didn't put up a struggle.

"Paulette," Dana said when they approached her. "I just wanted to say hello and introduce you to my friend, Al Bruno."

"Hello, Dana. How nice to see you again," Paulette said politely, then looking up at Bruno, she turned on a dazzling smile and grabbed hold of his hand. "And I'm delighted to meet you, Detective Bruno."

"It's nice to meet you," Bruno told her, disengaging his hand from her grasp. "Which way is the television set?"

Paulette smiled at him again. "Right through that door." She pointed to a door between the bar and the buffet tables. Bruno nodded and took off like he was carrying the ball into the end zone.

"Very attractive man," Paulette commented, watching Bruno's broad frame disappear through the doorway to the library. "Are you having a serious relationship with him?"

"Sometimes," Dana countered, looking directly

into her cold gray eyes. "How did you know he was a detective?"

"I've seen his name and photograph in your newspaper," Paulette told her, "in connection with some sort of crime he was investigating. You and he must have a lot in common, both being investigators."

"Sometimes," Dana said again.

"This reception seems a little out of your area," Paulette continued. "I was surprised to see you here."

"Just doing a favor for a co-worker," Dana said. "I was hoping to meet Mrs. Wright. Is she here today?"

The question did nothing to disturb Paulette's cool demeanor. "No. As soon as the cool weather starts, Mrs. Wright travels to a warmer climate—" she hesitated "—for health reasons."

"So I've heard," Dana replied.

Paulette sighed and without excusing herself moved past Dana to talk to a group of other guests that were heading toward the buffet table.

Dana shrugged and decided that since she was so close to the food, she would eat something. Ordinarily, she would have waited for Bruno, but she knew if the football game was good, she might not see him for a while. She picked up a sparkling white plate and made her way down the line, taking small samplings of fruit, cheese, and salads.

With her plate filled, Dana walked up to the front of the room again, and took a seat at a table near the doorway to the foyer. From her seat, she could see the sweeping staircase and some of the other paintings that were hung on the walls adjacent to it. Dana twisted her head and saw that the butler was still at his post, standing straight and tall, and looking very bored.

Dana picked up a fork and ate. The food was delicious. After a few moments, she was joined at the table by Dick and Jane. They were a husband and wife team who hosted a radio talk show on one of the local stations.

The fact that their first names corresponded with the characters in the first grade reading books that had once dominated the public school systems gave them instant recognition with older listeners. Their show was very popular. Listeners called in asking questions and making comments about civil affairs and life in general.

Dana hated talk shows, so she had never actually heard one of their broadcasts, but she knew Dick and Jane. Like Dana, they loved art and were staunch supporters of the gallery that occasionally displayed Dana's work. They had even worked on a few benefits together.

"Hi Dana," Dick said cheerfully. "How's the chow?"

"It's great."

"You look so pretty in that color," Jane gushed in the soft mellow voice that enthralled her listeners. Dana glanced down at the plain navy blue dress she was wearing, hardly a fashion statement, but she smiled and accepted the compliment. Jane was middle-aged and plump, with blond curly hair and rosy cheeks. She had a flowered dress that looked like it was Hawaiian in origin.

Dick was more than plump and reminded Dana of her lovable and crazy investigator, Bob. He was dressed in a conservative dark suit, but his tie matched his wife's dress, a definite fashion statement.

The three of them chatted as they ate their buffet lunches.

"Where's Bruno?" Jane asked.

"In the library watching the football game."

"There's a television in there?" Dick asked, dropping his fork on his empty plate. Almost instantly, a waiter appeared and whisked away the dish. Just as quickly, Dick excused himself and dashed across the room toward the library.

"Men and football," Jane said. "I hate the game myself."

"It's too slow for me," Dana agreed. "Basketball is my game."

Charles Wright with Paulette in tow walked past them toward the podium. "It must be getting close to speech time," Jane said.

"Yes," Dana agreed, watching as Charles and Paulette put their heads together and talked softly. Something was definitely going on between them, Dana thought.

Then, Paulette tapped on the microphone to make sure it was working and spoke into it.

"On behalf of Mr. Wright, I want to thank you all for coming today. In a few minutes, our candidate is going to outline his new education policy, and then you reporters will have an opportunity to ask questions. We do ask that you wait until Mr. Wright has given you all the details of his program before you ask your questions. So, if you haven't eaten yet, get a plate and a drink from the bar and find a seat. We'll begin in just a few minutes."

Bruno came up with a plate full of food and sat down next to Dana. He looked very grumpy. "The Bears must be losing," Dana said.

"Big time," Bruno said. "Hi, Jane."

"Did you see Dick?" she asked.

"Yeah. When I told him the score, he headed straight for the bar."

Jane swiveled around in her chair to see if Bruno was telling her the truth.

"Did you see any photos of you-know-who?" Dana whispered to Bruno.

"No." Bruno looked up and out toward the foyer. "But who needs pictures—tall redhead with a knockout figure dressed in emerald green coming down the stairs. Just like Scarlett O'Hara."

"What?" Dana thought Bruno was making a joke, but then she looked up and saw that he was simply describing the woman who was indeed sweeping down the stairs.

Dana held her breath watching the scene unfold. Paulette had returned to the microphone and was introducing Charles Wright. The guests had fallen quiet and focused their attention on the front of the room.

The redhead in the emerald green dress stood at the top of the steps, timing her arrival at the precise moment that Charles stepped up to address the gathering.

The candidate started to speak, and then stopped as the crowd murmured their acknowledgment of the woman's presence. Charles and Paulette both turned to see what the distraction was and Dana saw a look that resembled panic pass over their faces.

"Good afternoon, everyone." The gorgeous redhead spoke in a strong lilting voice. "I'm Madeline Wright and I'd like to welcome you all to my home. I trust you're having a pleasant time."

To his credit, Wright recovered quickly and rushed forward to escort his wife down the stairs and into the ballroom. "Darling," he exclaimed with true surprise. "I didn't think you'd feel up to joining us today."

Paulette rushed back to the microphone. "Ladies and gentlemen, Mrs. Wright has surprised us by returning early from her trip. We're delighted that she could join us. And just in time to hear her husband's views on the education issues that are so important to all of us."

"Good recovery," Dana said grudgingly.

"The wife or the mistress?" Jane whispered.

"Both," Dana whispered back.

The crowd fell silent again as Charles Wright put on his best campaign smile and ushered his wife to a seat near the podium.

FOURTEEN

AFTER THE SUNDAY-AFTERNOON press reception, Dana had filed a story on Charles Wright giving him the publicity he sought for his views on the State's educational system.

Of course the story had also mentioned the surprising appearance of the candidate's wife. This item had delighted her editor and frustrated Bernie. "Damn," he said, appearing in front of Dana's desk on Monday morning. "I should have been there."

"And according to Bruno, the football game was a disappointment too."

"Right," Bernie agreed. "But all that aside, the unexpected appearance of Mrs. Wright is the most exciting thing that has happened in this election campaign. I'm going to go out there today and try to interview the lady."

Later that afternoon, Bernie called Dana and reported that he had spent the better part of the day hanging out at the Wright mansion, but had not been able to speak to Madeline. "I think maybe the candidate whisked her off again."

"Like he did yesterday at the reception," Dana said. "Wright finished his speech and when it was obvious that the reporters had more questions about Mrs. Wright and her supposed health problems than about his views on education, he thanked everyone for coming, took his wife by the arm and ushered her back upstairs. Then, Paulette thanked everyone for coming and dismissed us."

"Strange behavior indeed," Bernie mused.

"So now what?" Dana asked.

"Like I said before, this is the most exciting thing that's happened in this campaign. The press is going to keep after Wright until we get some straight answers about his marriage and his wife."

"Some people think he's having an affair with Paulette Mason."

"I know. The thing is, a busted marriage won't necessarily keep him out of the Governor's Mansion, but the way he's acting now might. Start trying to cover things up and people just get more curious to know what's going on."

Dana laughed. His assessment of the situation was right on target. "Keep me posted," she said as they ended their conversation.

The rest of the day was spent with the staff meetings and phone calls necessary to keep Globe Investigations from falling behind in its caseload.

As she worked, Dana's thoughts kept drifting back to Charles and Madeline Wright and their possible connection to Leona Rosetti. She had to find out if Madeline Wright had talked to Leona. Actually, her instincts kept telling her that Madeline had talked to Leona. Proving it was another matter.

"Somebody got to Madeline," Wright had said. There were other ways to interpret that statement, but Dana's version was that Madeline had told the family secrets and someone was trying to blackmail Wright. Add that to the fact that Leona was murdered and her tape recorder was missing and one could assume there was a connection.

Last night, after the reception, Dana had almost shared her theory with Bruno. He was a good detective because he was both intelligent and objective, able to process information quickly and logically. Then she remembered that Bruno had not even bothered to ask Milecki to meet with her, nor had he offered any valuable insights into the unexpected appearance of Madeline Wright and the reactions of Charles and Paulette.

The bottom line was that Bruno didn't care about the case she was investigating. Bruno was too involved with the Royal Flush case and to be fair, she couldn't blame him. Crescent Hills and Pine Grove City were not the types of cities that were frequented by serial killers. Having this killer operating in these areas was both unusual and frightening.

Dana knew that a computer search showed that other cities had reported a rash of similar killings over the last few years that remained unsolved.

"If it's the same killer, the cards are a new addition," Bruno had told her. "Or it's a new wacko who wants to discourage homeless people from coming to this area."

Based on the fact that the killer was finding victims at an alarming rate, it seemed that the homeless were still hanging out in Crescent Hills and Pine Grove City.

One of *The Globe* feature writers had suggested that the police should round up all the derelicts and keep them in protective custody. If the killer couldn't find any victims, he might move on to another area.

Although Bruno would never admit it, Dana thought he silently applauded the reporter's suggestion. Bruno would rather be smeared with honey and staked out on an anthill than bestow a compliment on a reporter. Of course, Dana knew that underneath Bruno's tough exterior dwelled the soul of a poet. She had detected that early in their relationship and it was one of the things that had intrigued her.

Before leaving for her second job at Peaceful Pines, Dana called the hospital and inquired about Helen Johnson.

"No change," a nurse told her.

Sam had been there again over the weekend. He said after a few minutes, Helen had seemed more confused and rang for the nurse, who promptly shooed him out of the room.

Okay, Dana told herself as she settled in behind her desk at Peaceful Pines. Tomorrow I go back to the Wright mansion and try to talk to Madeline. If she's not available, maybe that bored butler or one of the other servants can tell me something. Tonight, I work the case from this end.

A few minutes later, Rocky greeted Dana through the window of the reception desk. "Good afternoon, Dana," he said politely. "How are you?"

"Can't complain," Dana told him. "How are things with you?"

"Good. Got a letter from my grandson today. Pictures of the bambinos too."

"How nice for you. Do you have many grandchildren?"

"Just two from my daughter, Angelina. She's in heaven with her mama now. Her boys are good boys. They are grown up men now. They live in California, work for the movies, make big money. That's how I live here. They pay for me."

"I see. So the bambinos are your great-grandchildren?"

"That's right. Michael has twin girls. Brian is not married yet. How about you? Are you available? I could fix you up with Brian next time he comes here to visit me."

Dana laughed. "Well, thank you, Rocky, but I'm not available."

"That's what I thought. The pretty girls are always taken."

Erna came across the lobby and tapped Rocky on the shoulder. "Rocky, you belong in the dining room. Your supper is going to get cold."

"Feed it to the dogs," he said with a smile.

"You are an old dog, and you must eat. You need your strength to keep up with all your girlfriends."

Rocky thought that was very amusing and Erna turned him in the direction of the dining room and gave him a gentle shove. After he was out of sight, Erna entered the office and stood in front of Dana.

"He's quite a character, isn't he?" Dana asked.

Erna nodded, but didn't return Dana's smile. Her serious look made Dana uncomfortable. "So who are you?" the stout woman asked suddenly.

"I'm Dana Summers. I work for a temporary agency. Like Mr. Templeton told you last week, I'm taking Janet's place for a few weeks."

"You are a policewoman," Erna said.

Dana was surprised by her statement. "No, I'm not."

"Then who are you?"

"I just told you," Dana replied evenly.

"No. It is not a true story. I talk to Janet all the time. We are friends. If she were going to take a vacation she would tell me. I called her now and she said that Templeton gave her time off as a bonus. Templeton would never do that. He's too cheap."

Dana held her ground. "Well, I'm sorry to disappoint you, but I'm not a policewoman."

Suddenly, Erna's face crumbled and Dana thought she would start to cry. "I apologize to you. Please forget what I have said. I am just a foolish woman."

"Why do you think Templeton would bring in a policewoman?"

"Because one of my lovely ladies was murdered here and now another is in the hospital and will never come back. I am afraid for everyone here. If you are not a policewoman, you must leave here and never come back." Erna turned and walked swiftly from the office.

Dana thought about going after her, but a kitchen worker arrived with Dana's dinner on a tray.

While she ate the roast beef and mashed potatoes delivered to her, Dana wondered if Erna had told the police anything useful. While the lobby was still empty, she dialed Bruno's cell phone number and he answered after two rings.

"Bruno, I need a favor."

"Who is this?"

"The receptionist at Peaceful Pines, and I don't have time to argue."

"Okay." Bruno sighed. "I'm on my way to a murder scene, so I'm a little pressed for time myself."

"I'm sorry. I'll talk to you later."

"It's okay. You have three miles to plead your case. Shoot."

"I really need to talk to Sergeant Milecki. Can you arrange it?"

"When you say talk, you mean pump him about the case you're working on."

Dr. Mary came into the office and smiled at Dana. She went right to work setting up her medical supplies. Apparently the residents had finished eating.

"That's right, sir." Dana's voice had become polite and impersonal.

"Someone just walked in on you?"

"Right again."

"Good, then you won't cuss me out when I decline your request."

The residents were beginning to line up again, waiting to be examined by Dr. Mary. Dana smiled and waved at them. "Of course I won't, but don't be hasty. Think about it first. I would be ever so grateful if you could help me out."

Bruno laughed. "Meet me on the jogging track in the morning. We can talk about it over breakfast. See you, sweets."

Bruno clicked off his phone, and for the next hour or so, Dana helped Dr. Mary with her patients.

When the last of the residents had been examined and sent on their way, Dr. Mary began packing up her bag.

"Did you know Leona Rosetti?" Dana asked.

"Oh, such a smart lady," Dr. Mary exclaimed. "And always full of questions. When those political people were here the rest of us just listened to their speeches and believed what they told us, but not Leona. She made them explain things in plain English."

"I understand she used to be a newspaper reporter, and always carried a tape recorder."

"Well, yes. She interviewed me one time and tried to sell my story to a big magazine, but they weren't interested."

"So, you really are a cop," a male voice said.

Dana spun around and saw that Peter Hogan was leaning through the window over the reception desk.

Dr. Mary waved in his direction. "Hello, Peter. What did you say?"

"He said it's time you went into the lounge and relaxed," Dana told her quickly. "You saw quite a few patients tonight."

"Yes. I am tired."

Dana held the door open for Dr. Mary. When the elderly woman was on her way down the hall, Dana leveled a severe look on Peter. "You must have been talking to Erna."

"Hey, don't get mad. I was just kidding. Erna was really shook up, but I told her you were much too pretty to be a cop." He gave her an engaging smile. "Of course, now I'm wondering how you knew Leona and heard about her tape recorder?"

"I didn't know her," Dana said, truthfully. "But I've been hearing a lot of stories about her."

"From the old folks?"

"Yes." This time Dana was lying, and she decided to take it one step further. "Someone said that she was murdered because of something she had on tape. Have you heard that one?"

Hogan stiffened and his smiling, casual manner

changed abruptly. "No. And let me warn you, Dana. Don't believe anything these old folks say. Some of them aren't sure of their own names."

Bull's-eye, Dana thought as Peter Hogan pushed himself away from the counter and hurried away from her. Mr. Peter Hogan definitely knows something about Leona and her tape recorder. Although she may have pushed her luck a little too far, and probably damaged her cover at Peaceful Pines, she had finally learned something useful and come up with a brand-new suspect.

FIFTEEN

THE NEXT MORNING, Dana slept through her alarm. She struggled out of bed and turned on the coffee pot, then while it was brewing, took a shower and washed her hair. Instead of blowing it dry, Dana fluffed her curls with a brush, one of the advantages of her recent haircut was that it could air-dry and still look presentable. She wrapped herself in a robe and went off to the kitchen to drink some coffee.

Dana's apartment was a one-bedroom in a two-story building with four apartments, two on each floor. The building was only a few years old, and Dana's place on the second floor was spacious and modern.

There was a large bedroom with its own bath, a living room with an alcove of bay windows where she stored her art supplies and painted whenever she got a chance. A powder room for guests was nestled between the living room and a small dining room. The kitchen was a good size with a breakfast bar, oak cabinets and modern appliances.

Dana was a good cook. Having grown up on a farm in southern Illinois, she had learned her way around the kitchen at an early age.

Her parents and brothers still worked the farm, and there was much about that life that Dana envied. Yet, once she had finished college, she only returned home for short visits and holidays. She missed her family, especially her mom, but her life in Crescent Hills was so full and busy, she didn't have much time to dwell on the things she'd left behind or to cook meals in her lovely modern kitchen.

Bruno kept saying when they got married, he'd quit the police force and they'd buy a farm in the country and live a peaceful, steady life like her parents. Maybe they would, someday.

Dana was sitting at the breakfast bar, thinking about the decision she had made just before falling asleep last night, when the doorbell rang, then rang again, and again.

There was only one person who stood in the hallway and kept pushing the bell over and over. Dana opened the door and Bruno jogged through it in a gray running suit. His dark curls were covered by the hood of his jacket and he was wearing wraparound mirrored sunglasses. He ran past Dana into the kitchen and helped himself to a cup of coffee, all the time jogging in place.

Dana came after him, and sat down at the counter again. "Are you trying to make me feel guilty?" she asked.

Bruno stopped jogging and took a sip of his coffee. "Not at all. I love abuse. That's why I'm always making dates with you, so you can stand me up." He whipped off the sunglasses. "Look into these eyes, they are the eyes of a man who loves abuse, the perfect man for Dana Sloan, super sleuth." He began to jog in place again.

Dana burst out laughing. "I'm sorry, I slept through my alarm. I didn't stand you up on purpose. Now why don't you stand still, you're vibrating my china."

Bruno stopped jogging and sat down at the counter next to Dana. She kissed him on the mouth and got up and poured herself more coffee.

"So what happened last night? The old folks wear you out?"

"As a matter of fact, they did. And to make matters worse, there's a rumor circulating through the staff that I'm a policewoman."

"Good, then you can give up the undercover work and spend the night with me."

"I did get some information that might be important," Dana told him, ignoring his invitation. "Did you arrange for me to meet with Milecki?"

"He was at the homicide scene with me last night, but we were a little too busy trying to figure out how we're going to catch this lunatic who's killing people in both our districts."

"You don't have any good leads?"

"I wouldn't say that."

"Then you're making progress on the case."

"Forget it, sweetheart. I'm not telling you so you can blab it to your editor."

"Okay, fine," Dana said as she took Bruno's coffee

cup and put it in the sink. "Let's go." She pulled at his arm until he came off the stool and began leading him through the apartment to the front door.

Bruno was laughing and letting her have her way, or she would never have been able to move him. When they got to the front door, he turned around and stood against it, keeping Dana from opening it. "I love it when you get tough with me." He pulled her into his arms and kissed her.

Dana responded, then pulled away from him. "I don't have time for this, Bruno. I've got to drive out to the Wright mansion this morning."

Bruno kept her captive in his strong arms. "Forget him, and I'll tell you what the new lead is on the Royal Flush case."

Dana let him kiss her again. "Okay. What's the new lead?" she asked with a smile.

"The playing cards on last night's victim were a different type of card."

Dana looked at him curiously. "So what?"

"There have been seven victims, four were stabbed, three were shot. The one consistency in the crimes, other than the fact the victims were all homeless men, has been the cards found on each victim. The first four victims had Royal Flushes from the same deck: Diamonds, Spades, Hearts and Clubs. Victim number five gets a new deck and a Diamond flush; number six has Spades. Last night's victim had Diamonds again. We backtracked and found that the cards on the last two victims came from a different brand of cards entirely."

Dana frowned at him. "So, you've got a serial killer with more than one brand of cards, or a copycat killer."

Bruno nodded and let go of Dana. "Right. It's not much, but it's something new to work on. It's the little details that sometimes catch a killer."

"You're right," Dana agreed. "That's why I need to talk to Milecki. I have one little detail to share with him on the Rosetti case."

"And that is?"

"You can sit in on our meeting, and I'll tell you both at the same time. Now, you've got to go so I can get dressed."

"Can I stay and watch?"

"You can stay out here and call Milecki and arrange that meeting."

Bruno looked like he might consider doing it, when his beeper sounded. He pulled it out of his pocket and read the display. "See you later, toots."

He gave Dana a quick kiss, and then hurried out the door. Dana ran for the bedroom to get dressed.

SIXTEEN

DANA PULLED her midnight-blue Mustang into the circular drive of the Wright mansion. With any luck, Charles and Paulette would be on the campaign trail, and Madeline Wright would be home alone. If not, Dana had an alternative plan that might be just as good.

She rang the doorbell, and after a few minutes, the butler opened the door. She flashed her press card and her brightest smile at him. He nodded, but didn't smile back. Undaunted, Dana asked to see Mrs. Wright.

"I'm sorry, Mrs. Wright is not at home," the butler said without expression.

"Is she out of town?" Dana asked.

"No."

"Well, do you know when she'll be back?"

"No."

"Do you know where she went?"

"Mrs. Wright left the house sometime last night. She did not tell me where she was going, or when she would return."

"You're very professional," Dana said. "Have you worked here long?"

"Yes, Miss. And I plan to continue working here. Is there anything else?"

Dana decided to go for broke. "Yes, actually there is. I'm investigating a murder and I need to ask you a few questions."

"I'm sure I couldn't help you."

"Look," Dana told him in a firm voice. "The gentleman I was here with on Sunday is a homicide detective. Now, you can either answer my questions here and our conversation will remain confidential, or my friend can arrange for you to answer the questions down at the police station. Then, being a newspaper reporter, I would have to report that the butler of the candidate for governor was..."

The butler held up his hand to cut her off, then gave her a menacing look, and stepped forward and closed the door softly behind him. "What can I help you with?"

Dana opened her handbag and withdrew a photo of Leona Rosetti. She showed it to the butler. "Has this woman ever visited here and talked to Mrs. Wright?"

The butler nodded. "Yes. About two weeks ago."

"Was she alone?"

"Someone drove her here and waited in the car while she spoke to Mrs. Wright."

"What kind of car was it?"

"A black Ford sedan. The man had light brown hair and a beard."

"How much time did she spend with Mrs. Wright?"

"I don't recall. It was a warm day and they talked in the garden. I left to run errands and when I came back she was gone and Mrs. Wright was back in her room."

Suddenly, the front door swung open and Charles Wright peered out at them. "What is going on out here, Henry?" he asked curtly.

Dana rushed forward and extended her hand. "Why Mr. Wright, how nice to see you. I'm having some car trouble and your butler was kind enough to come out and see if he could help me."

Henry quickly picked up Dana's lead. "However, once the young lady described the noise, I realized that I couldn't help. I've advised her to call a mechanic."

"I see. Well, come on inside then, Miss Sloan. You can use my telephone."

"Thank you."

The butler made a hasty exit and Dana slipped by Charles Wright and into the house. "I suppose you've come looking for Madeline," Wright said.

"No," Dana replied. "I was on my way to Pine Grove police station to meet with Sergeant Milecki, and I guess I got turned around, then the car started making a weird noise, so..."

Wright nodded. "Well, I'm sorry to disappoint you, Miss Sloan. As we've told all the members of the press who called or stopped by, Madeline is not giving interviews. Her health simply won't allow it. You can use the phone in my study. This way, please."

Wright's manner remained curt and guarded. Dana followed him to the study where Paulette was sitting at a desk, sipping a cup of coffee. She and Dana exchanged greetings. Wright explained about Dana's car and her need to use the telephone.

"Don't you have a cell phone?" Paulette asked pointedly.

"Yes, but it doesn't seem to be working properly this morning," Dana told her. "I guess it's just going to be one of those days."

Wright motioned to the telephone that was on the desk and Dana smiled and moved toward it. She would have to follow through with the charade. She punched in the number to her office and Marianne answered.

"Good morning, Globe Investigations."

"Maury," Dana said. "I'm at Charles Wright's house and my car is acting up. It's making a clanking noise. Any ideas?"

Dana had called Marianne earlier on her cell phone to tell her what she was planning to do instead of coming to the office. Being a clever girl, Marianne realized at once that her boss was bluffing. "Have you checked the gas gauge?" she said with a soft giggle.

"Well, no. I didn't even think of that. I'll do that and try it again. Thanks so much. If it doesn't work, I'll call you back and you can send the tow truck."

Dana hung up the phone and looked over at Wright who was sitting in an expensive winged-back chair, looking over some papers. "Well, he gave me something to try. I'll just run out and see if it works. Thanks so much for the use of the phone."

Dana headed for the door. Wright rose from the chair and walked her out to the foyer and opened the door for her in time to see Bruno's unmarked squad car squeal to a stop in front of the porch.

Bruno jumped out of the car, slamming the door behind him. A uniformed officer got out of the car on the other side.

"Well, it seems I have more company," Wright said.

"Bruno, what are you doing here?" Dana asked in a threatening tone. She should not have mentioned that she was coming out here this morning. Bruno walked deliberately up the steps, while the uniformed cop remained standing next to the car. "Charles, you remember Detective Bruno from the reception, Sunday."

"Yes, of course." Wright extended his hand.

Bruno ignored Wright's outstretched hand. He flashed his badge at the candidate. "I'm afraid this is official business, sir. Can we go inside?"

"Is something wrong?"

"I'm afraid so. Can we step inside, please?"

"Of course," Wright said, quickly leading the way through the still open door and on to his study.

Dana tried to follow right along with them, but

Bruno blocked her entrance to the study. "No reporters allowed," he told he firmly. The door to the study closed leaving Dana outside in the foyer.

Dana had to act quickly. On Sunday she had used a small powder room in the hallway adjacent to the study and she had just seen another entrance to it inside the study.

The butler had conveniently disappeared and Dana rushed into the tiny bathroom and concealed herself behind the partially open door that accessed the study. She was just in time to hear Bruno deliver his news to Wright.

"I have some bad news for you, Mr. Wright."

Dana could see the room from the space between the wall and the door. Paulette jumped up and rushed to the candidate's side.

"What's happened?" Wright asked in a strong voice.

"I'm sorry to tell you that your wife was found dead this morning, the apparent victim of a homicide." Bruno paused, waiting for the news to sink in.

Charles staggered forward, seemingly shocked and Paulette grabbed his arm to steady him.

"That's impossible," Wright said hoarsely. "There must be some mistake."

Bruno shook his head. "No mistake, sir. She was murdered."

Wright collapsed into the nearest chair. Paulette sprang forward to confront Bruno. "Where? How?"

"She was shot to death in the apartment of a man named Peter Hogan. Do you know him?"

Wright shook his head in a negative reply and Paulette, taking a cue from him, did the same.

"I don't understand," Wright mumbled. "Who is this Peter Hogan?"

"Apparently, he was someone who knew a great deal about you, Mr. Wright." Bruno reached in his pocket and took out a cassette tape and held it up for Wright to see.

Wright stared at the tape, but didn't say anything.

"You'll have to identify your wife's body, and then I'd appreciate it if you'd come to the station to answer some questions."

Paulette rushed forward to confront Bruno. "Are you arresting him?"

"Not at this time," Bruno replied calmly. "But I suggest you contact Mr. Wright's attorney."

Charles Wright nodded, seeming to have gotten back in control. "Just let me get my coat. Paulette, you'd better stay here and make the necessary phone calls." He turned and walked out into the hallway. Paulette ran after him.

Bruno started to follow, but Dana emerged from the powder room and grabbed his arm. "What about Peter Hogan?" she asked urgently.

Bruno's dark eyes filled with anger. "Eavesdropping, Miss Sloan?"

Dana ignored the questions. "Bruno, he works at Peaceful Pines."

"I know. My guys are already staked out there, hoping he'll show up. He's disappeared."

"That tape you talked to Wright about probably came from Leona's tape recorder. Did you find it in Hogan's apartment?"

"Look, Dana, I'd love to stay and chat, but I'm kind of busy right now." When Dana didn't move, Bruno lifted her up and set her out of his way.

Dana followed him out onto the porch. Paulette and Charles were already outside. They were speaking in low tones.

Dana grabbed Bruno's arm again. "Bruno, answer me. Did you find Leona's tape recorder?"

Bruno pulled out of Dana's grasp. Charles Wright looked at him. "I'm ready, Detective."

As the men started down the steps, Dana bounded down alongside them. The uniformed officer opened the back door of the squad car for Wright. Paulette stood on the porch watching. Dana headed for her own car, but Bruno came after her and this time, he grabbed hold of the collar on her coat, abruptly stopping her in her tracks. "And where do you think you're going?" he whispered.

"With you of course. You don't think I'm going to just let you waltz out the door with the biggest news story of the year, do you?"

"This is a police matter. Reporters are not invited."

"Quit being a jerk, Bruno. I'm tagging along on this one."

"No, you're not."

"You can't stop me. Freedom of the press, remember. I'll see you at the morgue."

"Not likely," Bruno said menacingly. "I'll be inside, and I'm issuing orders to bar all reporters, especially you."

Bruno turned and hurried to the police car. Paulette was still standing on the porch looking at Charles Wright through the back window of the car. As Bruno got in and drove off, Paulette ran into the house and slammed the front door.

Dana got into her car and started the engine. The tires of her Mustang squealed on the driveway as she drove away muttering unkind words about Detective Al Bruno.

SEVENTEEN

BOB AND MARIANNE WERE in the reception area of Dana's office having a good-natured discussion.

"Forget it, Bob. I'm not going out with your brother-in-law."

"Give me six good reasons," Bob demanded as Dana came flying through the door.

"Marianne, I need you to type up these notes right away and send them to the city desk." Marianne took the notebook Dana held out. "And call Sam and tell him I'm back. Oh, and call Peaceful Pines and tell Templeton I'm running late, but he should stay there until I arrive. I need to talk to him."

Marianne was already dialing the phone. Bob followed Dana into her office. "So what gives, Dana? Do the cops think Wright killed his wife?"

"So far he's just being held for questioning. Did you get the information I called you about?"

"It's there on your desk." Bob indicated the notes printed neatly on a yellow legal pad. Dana picked it up and quickly scanned the notes.

"Are you sure this is accurate?"

Bob nodded his blond head. "I double-checked, Dana. The desk clerk and restaurant hostess swear that Madeline Wright was at that Florida resort on the night Leona Rosetti was murdered. And the airlines confirmed that she only returned to Pine Grove City the morning of Wright's reception."

"That brings me right back to Peter Hogan," Dana said. "Although, Madeline could have been pulling the strings, even from Florida."

Sam entered the office and gave Bob a dismissive look. Bob hurried out, closing the door behind him.

"Has Wright been formally charged?" he asked.

"No. His lawyers are screaming their heads off, and there's no physical evidence to link him to the crime. I think they'll have to release him."

"Poor bastard, even if he's innocent, this is bound to hurt him at the polls. Did you get to hear the tape?"

Dana laughed. "Are you kidding? Bruno wouldn't let me within twenty feet of the interrogation room."

"But you found out what was on it?"

"No, but I'm sure it was Leona's tape. They found her recorder and the case with her initials on it in Hogan's closet. They also found evidence that indicates that Hogan may have been blackmailing Wright. By the way, we now owe your friend in the exhibit and evidence department season tickets to the Bears."

"It looks like Peter Hogan killed Leona."

"That's what the police think."

Sam looked at her curiously. "You don't agree?"

Dana shrugged and ran a hand through her short curls. "I don't know. Wright's butler confirmed that Leona was at the house and talked to Madeline, but there are too many unanswered questions here. The biggest one being what was Madeline Wright doing at Hogan's apartment? Were they in this together, or did she find out he had the tape and go there to get it back?"

"I guess we need to find Peter Hogan."

"Right, and that's why I'm going back to work at Peaceful Pines. Someone must know something about Hogan that can help me locate him."

"Don't do anything foolish," Sam warned. "Hogan is probably a killer."

"I'll be careful. I think you should go back to the hospital and talk to Helen again. Maybe she can help unravel this mess."

"I'll go over there when I leave you. I'll call you after I see her."

"Okay. Marianne is putting the story into the computer. Get someone to proof and edit it for me. I've got one more phone call to make, then I'm going out to Peaceful Pines to talk to Templeton."

Forty minutes later, Dana arrived at the retirement home to find police cars patrolling the grounds and the front lobby filled with people.

The elderly residents were milling around, looking out the window at the police cars and chattering nervously about Peter Hogan. Dana was amazed that the news had traveled there so quickly.

Dana dodged the residents who wanted to talk to her, and hurried down the corridor to John Templeton's office. He was waiting at the door for her.

"This just keep getting worse and worse," Templeton said. As Dana brushed past him he closed the door and hurried to sit behind his desk. Dana was already settled in one of the visitor's chairs.

"I need to see Peter Hogan's personnel file," Dana told him.

"Yes, of course. I already got it out for the police. I made a copy for you."

Templeton handed her a manila folder and Dana opened it and scanned its contents. There was an application, a report from a security company that had verified that Hogan had no arrest record or bad debts and the usual payroll deduction forms. "Is this all you've got?" Dana asked.

"Yes. As you can see he was checked out and approved for employment. And we've never had any complaints or anything registered against him. He was a good, dependable employee."

"All right, then what are your personal thoughts on Hogan?"

"Miss Sloan, I don't make a practice of socializing with the employees. I don't know anything about Peter Hogan other than what's in that file."

"Well, surely you talk to the residents from time to time. What did they think of Hogan?"

"I never heard anything but positive comments. The ladies in particular liked him."

"Someone I talked to earlier today told me that Peter Hogan drove Leona Rosetti to Charles Wright's mansion a few weeks ago. Why would Peter be the one to do that?"

Templeton's thin face went white. "Hogan was an orderly. He was not authorized to take the residents off the grounds."

"Then he did it on his own time, without your knowledge."

"I don't know. I suppose he could have. As I said, the ladies liked him quite well." Then he straightened up and talked in a firmer voice. "I hope you are not going to publicize that. It would indicate a serious breach of the care and security we give our residents."

Dana took a deep breath. "I can't promise you anything," she said sternly as she rose from the chair.

Templeton jumped up and hurried around the desk to open the door for her. "The police are coming to question me again. What should I tell them?" he asked.

"Tell them the truth," Dana advised. "I'm going to talk to Erna Schmidt and then I'll be working in the reception office. If you think of anything that can help me find Peter Hogan, call me immediately."

"I've told you everything I know about the man," Templeton insisted.

"I hope so," Dana told him.

Dana passed through the lobby again on her way to see Erna. The lobby and the reception office were both empty. She glanced at her watch. The daytime receptionist had young children and never stayed late. The residents must have been herded off to the dining room for their evening meal.

Like Templeton, Erna was waiting at the door to her office for Dana.

"Did you find out anything?" Dana asked.

"No. I called his old girlfriend and left the message you said. I also called the pool hall, and the tavern where he goes. No one has seen him, but I left the message there too."

"Thanks, Erna."

Dana had called Erna earlier and asked her to try and track down Hogan for her. Erna had agreed without asking any other questions. Now she looked at Dana with suspicion in her eyes. "So I was right about you," Erna said smugly. "You are a policewoman."

Dana smiled. "I'm an investigator."

"Sent here to find Leona's killer," Erna insisted.

"Yes," Dana admitted. "Look, someday I'll explain the whole story."

The voice of the activities director came over the P.A. system: "Tonight's movie will be shown in the first-floor lounge. It's a bright, romantic comedy starring Doris Day and Rock Hudson, called *Pillow Talk*. It will begin promptly at seven o'clock. Refreshments will be served."

"I'd better get to the reception office," Dana told Erna. "Call me if you hear any news about Hogan."

Erna nodded. Dana returned to the lobby in time to see the uniformed cop that had been with Bruno earlier turn the corner toward Templeton's office. Since Madeline Wright had been murdered in Crescent Hills, the Crescent Hills police were handling the case.

The next hour was quiet. The policeman left without even looking in Dana's direction. A few minutes later, Templeton hurried out the front door.

Dana's dinner tray was delivered as usual, but when Dana tried to question the kitchen worker, he said he had been instructed not to discuss anything with anyone, and left immediately.

Dana sat quietly and ate everything on the tray. Tonight's entrée was chicken and dumplings and it was really quite tasty. For dessert there was chocolate cake and although the frosting was a little too sweet, Dana polished off every crumb. The only thing she had eaten during the day was a powdered doughnut she had scrounged up at the police station.

The same kitchen worker returned to get Dana's empty tray, but once again hurried off without saying a word.

Dana was beginning to wonder why she was wasting her time sitting there at Peaceful Pines, when Dr. Mary and Rocky came into the lobby together. They were arguing.

"Go watch the movie, you old fool," Dr. Mary said.

"You watch it yourself, Missus. I have a right to walk around."

"You just want to hear what I'm going to tell the police, and it's none of your business."

"You're going to get yourself in big trouble. Like Leona and Helen," Rocky told her.

"I don't care," the elderly doctor retorted. "I have to tell them what I know."

Dana walked out of the office and approached them. They both looked at her and shut their mouths.

"Can you two come into my office?" Dana asked. "I'd like to talk to you."

They both nodded and followed Dana into the reception office. She closed the door.

Rocky smiled at Dana. "You want to know about Peter being a murderer?" he asked.

"You know that's not true, Rocky," Dr. Mary cried. "Dana, will you tell this old fool to leave me alone. I have to go out and speak to the police for a moment."

Dana patted her arm. "Look, Dr. Mary, I think that maybe you should tell me whatever it is you were going to tell the police."

Dr. Mary eyed Dana suspiciously. "You? Why should I tell you?"

"Because she is not really the receptionist," Rocky informed her. "She is a policewoman."

Dr. Mary took a step backward, obviously shocked by Rocky's declaration. "Oh," she said softly. "And you look like such a nice girl."

This time, Dana didn't deny it. "Any information you can give me will be kept confidential. Erna is helping me too."

"See, I told you," Rocky said. "She's a policewoman. Tell her what you know."

Dr. Mary still appeared skeptical, so Rocky nudged her, nodding for her to speak. "I was just going to tell them that I know that Peter is not a killer."

"How do you know?" Dana asked.

"Because Peter is a wimp," Rocky said loudly. "He could not kill a mosquito."

"Listen to me, Rocky," Dana told him, sternly. "Some people can appear to be very nice and still be killers."

"Oh, don't pay any attention to Rocky," Dr. Mary said. "He doesn't know a thing."

"I know a man who plays poker with women is a sissy," Rocky said stubbornly.

Dana glanced out into the lobby to be sure no one else had come in. "Dr. Mary," she said patiently. "Please, tell me what you know."

The old woman nodded and began to speak. "Sometimes, I have trouble sleeping so I sit in my rocker and look through the crack in my door. My room is across the hall from Leona and Helen's. On the night Leona died, I saw Peter go into their room and come out with Leona's case, the one she kept her tape recorder in. It made me very upset that he was stealing it, so I followed him to see where he was going. He took the case and left the building. I saw him get into his car and drive away. I knew how important that tape recorder was to Leona, and I got to thinking that maybe Peter hurt Leona or Helen in order to get it. So I went into their room to check on them. They were both sound asleep and fit as fiddles."

"And did you tell Leona about her tape recorder being stolen?" Dana asked.

Dr. Mary sighed and shook her head in a negative reply.

Rocky grinned at Dana. "Pretty stupid, huh?"

Dana ignored him. "Why didn't you tell her, Dr. Mary?"

"Because, young lady, I've been a doctor for longer than you have lived. I know better than to wake people out of a sound sleep to give them bad news. Besides there wasn't anything we could have done at that time of night."

"You could have reported it to one of the other staff members," Dana suggested.

"Then Peter would get fired, and she didn't want that," Rocky said. "He's a sissy, but the ladies like him."

Dr. Mary spoke again. "The next morning when I found out Leona had died during the night, I thought it didn't matter anymore."

"But what about when the police came and questioned everyone?" Dana persisted. "Why didn't you tell them, or tell Mr. Templeton?"

Rocky laughed. "Templeton is worse than a baby. We tell him nothing."

Dr. Mary nodded in agreement. "I knew that Peter didn't hurt Leona, and I felt if I told them about the tape recorder, he would be suspected and maybe even go to jail."

The front door opened and Dana heard someone walk into the lobby. She quickly escorted Dr. Mary and Rocky out of the office. Much to her surprise and annoyance, the person she found standing in the lobby was Bruno.

"What do you want?" Dana asked in a hostile tone.

"I want to talk to you."

Dr. Mary and Rocky stood silently as Dana walked up to confront Bruno. "Get lost," she yelled. She didn't wait for him to answer before walking back into the office. She closed the door and locked it.

Bruno leaned through the window to talk to her again. "Come on, honey. Cut me a little slack here. When I'm on duty, you're not my girlfriend, you're just another reporter."

Rocky and Dr. Mary walked up and stood beside Bruno. "I thought she was a policewoman," Rocky told him.

"Nice going, Bruno," Dana said angrily. "Now you've blown my cover."

Dr. Mary looked sternly at Rocky. "She is not a policewoman, and you made me tell her about Peter," she said accusingly.

Bruno spun around, suddenly very interested in what Dr. Mary had said. He took out his badge and showed it to her. "I'm Detective Al Bruno. What exactly have you told Miss Sloan?"

"I thought her name was Summers," Rocky said.

Dana banged out of the office and gave Bruno a shove. It didn't move him. "Nice going, Bruno," she whispered. "Have I told you lately that I hate your guts?"

Dr. Mary and Rocky exchanged bewildered looks.

"Rocky, I think we'd better go see the movie," Dr. Mary whispered.

Rocky agreed and took Dr. Mary's arm to lead her away, but Bruno stepped in front of them, blocking their way.

"Not so fast. You were going to tell me what you know about Peter Hogan."

"We never heard of him," Rocky said quickly.

Bruno tried a different tactic. "Now listen, old timer, I know this Hogan guy may be a friend of yours, but he's wanted for murder. If you know something you had better tell me."

Dana stepped between the elderly couple and Bruno. "Stop trying to frighten them, Bruno."

Bruno glared at her. "You stay out of this, Dana. It's a police matter."

"Really, young man," Dr. Mary said firmly. "You are never going to win her hand by using that tone of voice. A gentleman always speaks softly to a lady."

The telephone rang. Dr. Mary and Rocky sidestepped Bruno and hurried off. Dana ran back to the office and answered the phone.

"Good evening, Peaceful Pines," Dana said when she picked up the telephone. "Oh, hi, Sam." She paused to listen to what her editor had called to tell her. "You're kidding. Well, you have to admit the man has guts."

Bruno leaned through the window and listened openly to Dana's side of the conversation. She tried to close the window on him, but his broad shoulders were wedged into the opening, making it impossible to shut him out.

"How are things there?" Sam asked.

"I'll talk to you about that later," Dana replied, making a face at Bruno. "What happened at the hospital?" Again, she paused to listen. "Again? I guess communicating is just too difficult for her. Look, Sam, I have a very unwelcome visitor here, so I'll have to call you later." Dana and Sam ended their conversation.

"I take it that was your editor," Bruno said in a friendly tone.

"Yes. So why are you still here? Weren't you able to beat the truth out of the old couple?"

"Very funny." Then, Bruno shook his head and actually looked very contrite. "Okay, Dana. I apologize."

Dana turned her back on him and began walking around the office, straightening things that didn't need straightening, humming to herself as if no one else was around.

Bruno tried again. "Look, honey, I know you think Madeline Wright's death is connected to Leona's, and you're probably right. I can tell you this much. The tape we found in Hogan's apartment did belong to Leona."

Dana looked at him as if the news surprised her. "Sam just told me that Wright's opponent is demanding he withdraw from the governor's race, but Wright is standing firm. Says he'll run his campaign from a jail cell, if necessary."

"He's not in jail," Bruno admitted. "We had to release him."

"Really. Then I guess the tape wasn't too damaging."

"I'm not telling you what was on that tape. It's evidence."

Dana walked back to the window and attempted to close it again. Bruno cussed and foiled her attempt. "It was an interview that your friend, Leona, conducted with Madeline Wright. Ten minutes of a vindictive wife whining about a husband who neglects her. Apparently, Hogan thought the candidate would pay big bucks to keep his sterling image from being tarnished, so he killed the old girl to get the tape. Then Mrs. Wright had a change of heart and went to Hogan's apartment to get the tape, and he killed her too."

"Peter Hogan is not a killer," Dana told him.

"Is that what the old folks told you?"

"Yes, but I'd already decided that for myself. Look, Bruno, as much as I'd like to have both our cases tied up in a nice, neat package to pin on Peter Hogan, I don't think he killed anyone."

Bruno gave her a dazzling smile. "Fine. I respect your opinion. Now why don't you just close up this office and come home with me? We need some quiet time together."

"You're off your rocker if you think I've forgiven you for the way you treated me today," Dana said quietly.

"Look, honey, both of us are trying to do a job. Sometimes, that causes conflicts in our relationship, but you and I are great together. And we can't let our professional differences damage our personal lives."

Dana put her hands on her slim hips and stared at him. "That's the same speech I gave you a few weeks ago."

Bruno smiled at her again. "And you were so right."

"What about the meeting with Detective Milecki you promised to set up for me?" Dana asked.

"Come out here and give me a hug, and I'll call him right now and set it up for tomorrow."

"And you'll go with me to make sure he shares all his information on the case?"

Bruno sighed and nodded. Dana came out of the office and stepped into his open arms. She had to admit that Bruno's embrace always made her feel safe and secure. He held her against his chest and kissed the top of her curly head. "Between you and I, our kids are bound to have curls," he told her.

Before Dana could answer, Erna came into the lobby and cleared her throat to get their attention. Bruno released Dana.

"Erna, I'd like you to meet a friend of mine, Al Bruno."

"Nice to meet you," Bruno said.

Erna nodded.

"I'll wait for you in the car," Bruno told Dana.

"Great. You can use your car phone to make that call," she said pointedly.

Bruno turned and left the building.

Dana turned back to face Erna. "Everyone's at the movie. I thought I'd close the office for the night."

"He is nice-looking for a policeman," Erna said thoughtfully. "Are you serious with him?"

Dana shrugged. "I'm not ready to get married, if that's what you mean."

"Good. I got married once. It was a big mistake."

"What happened to your husband?"

"He is happy now without me to nag him."

"I'm sorry."

"Don't be. I am happy working here with these lovely old people."

"I know. Look, I don't know if I'll be coming back here. You have my number at my office and at home."

Erna nodded. “You will still try to help Peter? I know he is not a killer.”

“I don’t think so either,” Dana told her. “But I can’t help him unless I hear his side of the story.”

“I will call if I hear from Peter,” Erna promised.

EIGHTEEN

JACK SHEA PARKED HIS CAR in the lot next to the Sundown Lounge. It was a blue-collar neighborhood and this particular bar did most of its business in the mornings when the night-shift workers from the plastics factory across the street came in to unwind before going home to sleep.

Workers from the factory lined up at the bar every weekday morning. It used to be that on paydays wives would line up right behind the men coming off the night shift. The Sundown gladly cashed the worker's checks, and the wives were there to collect the bulk of the cash for groceries and other necessities.

In recent years, automatic payroll deposits had cut down on the paychecks cashed at the Sundown and the morning patrons now included as many female workers as men.

The bar also did a fair amount of business when the day shift ended at the factory. Those workers began drifting in about three in the afternoon and most had drifted out again by five or six.

It was now after nine, and on this weekday evening the Sundown Lounge only had a handful of patrons.

Most were seated at the bar watching television or quietly talking to each other.

The bartender was the owner and Jack Shea's cousin, Bill O'Brien. He was a congenial host who patiently listened to everything his customers cared to tell him. He was always sympathetic but never offered advice. Giving advice, he had learned years ago, was bad for business.

Jack walked in and stood by the door for a few seconds, waiting for his eyes to adjust to the dim interior of the bar. There were a number of empty tables scattered about and a few high-backed wooden booths against the far wall.

The bartender waved at Jack and motioned him over. "He's in the office," Bill told him quietly. "You want a drink?"

"Give me a draft," Jack replied.

With his beer in hand, Jack moved to a door next to the last booth in the row. It was marked with a sign that said "Private." Bill pushed a button under the bar and the automatic lock on the door clicked open. Jack hurried through the door, closing it behind him and hearing the lock click into place again.

The door accessed a short hall that led to a storeroom and O'Brien's private office. The office door was closed but it was not locked.

Jack entered the office. The only light came from a small lamp on a battered metal desk that held a stack of papers, an adding machine, and a telephone.

Peter Hogan was seated behind the desk fiddling

with the cord on the telephone. He looked up at Jack and relief flooded his face.

"Thanks for coming, Jack," Peter said.

"You look like crap," Jack replied. He sat down on the other side of the desk in a straight-backed chair and took a sip of beer before placing the glass on the desk.

"You have a woman murdered in your apartment and see how great you look," Peter told him.

"Sorry."

"Did you bring the money?"

"Yeah, but it's not much. We're always tapped out this time of the month. I had to empty the kids' piggy banks and take the coins to one of those automatic counters at the grocery store."

Jack reached into his jacket pocket and pulled out some folded bills. He handed them across the desk to Peter. "Sixty-five bucks."

"Thanks. I really appreciate it," Peter said.

"You're not going to get far on that."

"I know, but it's enough to buy a bus ticket to St. Louis. I got a friend there, a guy I was in the army with."

"Geez, Pete. The cops will be checking with all your friends."

"They won't know about this guy. They'll just be checking on people here. They call you yet?"

"No, but I figure it's just a matter of time before they do. Then, I'm going to have to lie and tell them I don't know where you are, or where you might go."

"Sorry."

"It's okay. What are friends for? So you want to tell me about it?"

"No. The less you know, the better. When the cops question you, you won't have to tell so many lies."

"The newspaper says they suspect you were blackmailing Charles Wright. Is there any truth to that?"

"Yeah."

"Man. This is like something out of the movies. My best friend involved in blackmail and murder. You didn't kill the woman, did you, Pete?"

"What do you think?"

"If I thought you did it, I wouldn't have broken open my kids' banks to help you."

"You and your cousin, Bill, are lifesavers. He's been letting me hide out here all day."

"He must have some dough stashed here, enough to get you farther away than St. Louis. California would be good."

"He offered some, but I didn't take it. With Lillian so sick, I know he needs every dime this place brings in."

"See," Jack said, smiling, "that's how I know you didn't kill anybody. You're a nice guy. Pretty stupid, sometimes, but nice all the same."

"I really stepped into it this time, Jack. I don't know how I'm going to get out of this mess. Trying to blackmail that guy was a big mistake."

"You think Wright followed his wife to your place and killed her?"

"I don't know, maybe."

"The cops let him go. You're their number one suspect."

"I know. I'm in a real jam."

"You got that right. Oh, by the way, I got a phone message for you. Some woman called the pool hall for you. Lefty took it and passed it on to me. I hope you can read his chicken scratching. It didn't make sense to me." Jack reached into his pocket again and brought out a cocktail napkin with some writing on it.

Peter took the napkin and moved it under the desk light to read it, while Jack took a long drink of his beer.

"It's from Erna."

"Who's Erna?"

"A nurse at Peaceful Pines, a great lady."

"What does she want?"

"Dana wants to help me. There are phone numbers to call."

"Who the hell is Dana?"

Peter shook his head and ran his hand down his beard. "The new receptionist. Erna kept telling me she was an undercover policewoman sent there to find out who killed Leona."

"Holy cow," Jack exclaimed, setting his beer down with a thud. "You can't call a cop. What is this Erna thinking?"

"I don't know. But Dana isn't a cop. She's that

newspaper reporter that does all those investigations for *The Globe.*"

Jack nodded. "The good-looking one with the curly hair?"

"Yeah. That's her."

"And she's the new receptionist at Peaceful Pines?" Jack asked in a skeptical tone.

"You remember the old girl that died there a week or so ago?"

"The one you were so upset about?"

"Right. Leona was once a hotshot reporter for *The Globe.* I think that's why Dana is investigating her death. I saw an article Dana wrote about Wright in the paper and it all clicked into place. She's at Peaceful Pines investigating Leona's death."

"I thought she died of natural causes."

"No."

Jack jumped to his feet. "She was murdered?"

"Yes. It's been kept quiet so as not to give Peaceful Pines any bad publicity."

"I don't believe this, Peter. Two murders? What the hell are you into?"

"Mud up to my eyeballs."

"Do you think this reporter really wants to help you? It could just be a trick."

"Not if the offer came through Erna. She and I are good friends. Maybe if I talk to Dana she can help me out of this."

"Maybe she'll help you right into a jail cell. I say get the hell out of town. You can call her from St.

Louis. I packed some clothes for you and Nadine packed you sandwiches, peanut butter and jelly. She said they would keep without spoiling."

"Did you check the bus schedules?"

"Yeah. There's a Greyhound leaving for Chicago at midnight. From there you can connect to almost anywhere. I'll drive you to the Oakhurst station. The cops may have the Crescent Hills station staked out." Jack grinned. "Wow. This is just like the movies."

Ten minutes later, Jack drove his car into the alley behind the Sundown. The back door opened and Bill came out and looked up and down the alley. Satisfied that it was safe, Bill motioned to Peter who was standing in the hallway outside the office.

"Good luck, Pete," Bill said as Peter brushed past him and ducked into Jack's car.

As the car pulled away, Bill closed the door and replaced the heavy metal bar across the inside of the door. Then, he hurried back down the hallway to the bar area where he still had a few customers nursing drinks and watching television.

NINETEEN

THE NEXT AFTERNOON, Dana and Bruno met Detective Sergeant Milecki at the Pine Grove City police station. He led them to a small room usually reserved for interrogations.

Milecki was a middle-aged man with a bald head and oversized, dark-rimmed glasses. He was as tall as Bruno and twice as wide, but his smile was genuine and disarming, making his size a little less intimidating. He greeted Dana warmly.

"Hey, Bruno," he said as they all took seats around a square table. "How'd an ugly ape like you get hooked up with a doll like this?"

"Don't let the sweet face fool you," Bruno told him. "She'll cut your heart out and serve it on crackers."

Milecki thought that was very amusing. Dana waited patiently until the detectives stopped chuckling before she spoke. "I'm sure Bruno explained that I'm looking into the death of Leona Rosetti. What can you tell me about the case?"

"The missing orderly," Milecki replied simply. "Now that Mrs. Rosetti's tape recorder and tapes have been recovered, I think it's pretty obvious."

"Perhaps," Dana said. "But what can you tell me

about the other people you questioned at Peaceful Pines?"

Milecki shrugged and pushed a file folder across the table to Bruno. "I've made copies of everything we had on the case. I'm now turning the copies over to a fellow officer. If you promise not to cut his heart out, I'm betting he'll let you look at them."

"Thank you," Dana said. "But I'd also like to know your personal take on the case, initially, that is, before the connection to Madeline Wright and Peter Hogan."

Milecki shrugged again. "Ordinarily, I don't discuss my cases with the media, but you've earned a good reputation for helping the police, that and your relationship with Bruno is the only reason I'm making an exception in this case." Dana smiled at him and waited for him to continue. "Initially, I thought Templeton killed her."

Dana stared at him, seeing her own image reflected in his thick glasses. "And his motive would have been?"

"Nothing concrete. I didn't get that far. It was just a gut reaction to the guy, something really sleazy about him."

Dana nodded. "I know what you mean. My editor and I thought the same thing. But there's got to be more than that."

"Yeah," Bruno agreed.

Milecki pointed at the file in front of Bruno. "There're a few references in the reports. Some of the staff mentioned that Templeton and the old woman didn't like each other. Apparently this Mrs. Rosetti was very outspoken and had told the guy off a few times about the way he treated some of the staff, specifically young female members of the staff."

"Sexual harassment?" Dana asked.

"A possibility I wanted to explore further," the detective replied. "Given Rosetti's connection to your newspaper, she could have represented a threat to Templeton and his position at Peaceful Pines. But with a serial killer on the loose, I didn't have the time to go back out there and make more inquiries."

"Well," Dana said thoughtfully. "Perhaps I will be going back to work at Peaceful Pines after all."

"A waste of time," Bruno declared. "Hogan's our guy in this case and in the murder of Madeline Wright. The sooner we get him, the sooner we can all concentrate our efforts on finding the lunatic that's trying to wipe out the county's homeless men."

"I agree," Milecki told Dana. "Hogan's motive is a lot stronger than the suspicion of hanky panky with Templeton and his female staff members."

"Look," Dana said making a quick decision. "Last night one of the residents at Peaceful Pines gave me some information that I'm going to share with you."

Dana repeated Dr. Mary's story about seeing Peter leave Leona's room with her tape recorder and then going into the room to find that Leona and Helen were both fine.

"He could have come back later and killed her after your Dr. Mary had left her post. As an employee, I'm sure he could slip in and out of the place without anyone seeing him."

Dana nodded. "It's a possibility," she admitted. She rose to her feet and both men stood as well. "Thank you for your help," she said, extending her hand to Milecki.

"You're welcome," Milecki took her hand and kissed it gallantly. "And if you want to talk some more, you just call me directly. We don't need this guy anymore." He shook his bald head in Bruno's direction.

Bruno pulled Dana's hand from the other cop's grasp and held onto it. "Thanks, Milecki. I'll be talking to you," Bruno said in a friendly tone as the two men shook hands.

"How about some lunch?" Dana asked when she and Bruno arrived at his car. "I'm buying."

"Then I'm eating," Bruno said. He helped Dana into the car and then went around to the other side and slid easily behind the wheel.

As they drove off, Dana reached over and pulled the file folder from the jacket pocket Bruno had stuffed it into. "Do you have to check in at the station?" she asked.

"I'll check in after lunch," Bruno said. "That way I won't get any bad news that might ruin my appetite."

Dana laughed. "It would have to be pretty bad to affect your appetite."

"What about you? You need to call your editor?"

"I'll see him after lunch." Dana opened the file and began to scan the reports Milecki had copied for her.

"Templeton ever make a pass at you?" Bruno asked suddenly.

"No, but then he wouldn't dare. He knew I was there investigating Leona's death."

"Lucky for him. What's the chump look like?"

Dana laughed again. "Like an undertaker, tall, thin, morose."

"First thing a cop learns, looks are deceiving."

"Same for a reporter," Dana agreed.

"You think Templeton could have killed your friend?"

"Actually," Dana replied, thinking aloud. "I can accept him in the role easier than Peter Hogan."

"What do you know that you're not telling me?" Bruno asked pointedly. "That story about the lady doctor seeing Leona alive after Hogan left her room isn't good enough. Like Milecki said, he could have come back any time that night and killed her. What other information do you have that makes you think he's innocent?"

"I don't have concrete evidence, Bruno. I'm just relying on my instincts. As you know, I do that quite a lot and am often right," Dana replied.

"Come on, Dana. I know you. You haven't been

hanging around that retirement home all week without getting some pertinent information. There's another reason you don't buy Hogan as the killer. What is it?"

"I just think that an old woman like Leona couldn't be considered much of a threat to a young guy like Hogan. His job at Peaceful Pines wasn't that important to him. On the other hand, a man like Templeton, in a position of authority with a high salary, might see the possible loss of his job as very significant."

"Good answer. It even makes sense," Bruno told her. He turned and looked at her. "But I'm betting you've got a few theories you're not sharing."

"I'm in the mood for something really fattening, like greasy hamburgers and deep-fried onion rings," Dana said. "Why don't we go to Big Lou's? It's close enough to the paper that I can walk to my office after lunch and burn off some of the calories."

"Are you ever going to tell me your real thoughts on all this?" Bruno persisted.

"Why should I? I told you about Dr. Mary's observations and you discounted them."

"If your only sources are those old folks at the home, they may not be too reliable. That's why they live in a supervised care facility."

"Good answer." Dana smiled and lightly punched his arm. "It even makes sense."

Bruno honked the horn at a pedestrian that was about to enter the crosswalk the car was approaching. The man quickly jumped back on the curb and

Bruno sped through the light that was turning from yellow to red.

Dana refrained from telling Bruno that he had just run a traffic light. Even when Bruno was in his personal car as he was today, he drove like he was in a police vehicle with the lights flashing and the siren blaring. She settled back in her seat and began reading the reports in Milecki's file.

By the time Bruno parked in the lot next to Big Lou's café, Dana had closed the file again. Most of the reports she had read so far said basically the same thing. Leona Rosetti was a feisty, outspoken woman but she was well-liked by the other residents and the staff. A few people had alluded to the fact that Leona was always asking questions and listening to the concerns of her peers as well as staff members at Peaceful Pines. On more than one occasion, she had gone to Templeton and asked him to rectify situations that had come to her attention through her interaction with various people.

Two of the staff members interviewed reported that Templeton sometimes made inappropriate remarks and got too "touchy-feely" with female workers. One of the staff told the police that Leona had noticed Templeton's behavior and told him to keep his horse in the barn or she would see to it that he and the horse were put out to pasture.

Apparently the contents of this report were the basis of the theory Milecki had shared earlier, but as he had also said, no follow-up interviews had been done to investigate the allegations further.

Big Lou's was still fairly quiet when Dana and Bruno arrived. It was a little early for the regular lunch crowd. Big Lou, who was actually an attractive middle-aged woman named Lucille, greeted Dana with a smile, and Bruno with a hug.

Lucille's husband was a retired police lieutenant and her café's booming business was due in part to the fact that all the cops in town ate there. Of course, the food was always fresh, hot, and generously piled on the plates, another important factor in the café's success.

"How's Clayton?" Bruno asked after Lou had settled them into his favorite booth and delivered two steaming mugs of coffee.

"He's better than nothin'," Lou replied. "I'm trying to teach him to cook, so he can help out around here sometimes, but it's like trying to milk an alligator."

Neither Dana or Bruno needed to look at a menu. Bruno ordered the special, which was meatloaf and mashed potatoes. Dana stuck by her original craving for a hamburger and onion rings.

This café had had a number of different owners over the past few years, but none had bothered to try to make it more than a place that people frequented when they were in a rush and the better restaurants were filled.

Lucille had changed all that. She had redecorated and rearranged the storefront, putting her own unique stamp on the place. The stainless steel and red leather had been replaced by white wood, flowered wallpaper, and frilly yellow curtains. The new decor reminded Dana of her mother's bright, warm country kitchen at the farm and Lou's menu was also reminiscent of home cooking.

"Hey," Bruno said, placing his hand over hers. "Now that I've bent the rules and helped you get information from Milecki, will you marry me?"

Dana smiled at him. Bruno proposed about once a month, and didn't seem too upset when she said she wasn't ready yet. "Someday I'll say yes, and you'll run the other way," she teased.

"Do you want me to get down on my knees right now?"

"Not unless you're planning on scrubbing the floor. And it looks like Lucille already did that this morning."

"So, what did you find in Milecki's reports?" Bruno asked, changing the subject again.

"Not a lot," Dana admitted. "But I will go back to Peaceful Pines tonight and talk to some of the staff again. If nothing else, it's given me a new thread to follow."

"What about the old gal in the hospital? Did you think to ask her about Templeton?"

"No, but I will. Although she hasn't been much help so far, but maybe it's because we haven't asked her the right questions yet."

"That's the trick," Bruno agreed. "Ask the right questions and you may get the right answers."

"That's what I'm thinking," Dana told him. "Like Leona's interview with Madeline Wright. I'd love to hear that tape."

"If that's a hint, you can forget it," Bruno replied with an engaging smile. "I already told you all you're going to hear."

"Which was about as helpful as a rubber crutch," Dana said.

"Are you ever going to marry me?" Bruno said, once again turning the conversation in a different direction.

"Probably."

"When?"

"Bruno, I'm in the middle of a murder investigation. Getting married isn't something I have time to think about right now."

"I'm working on the same case, remember? And then there's the other case I've got going. A serial killer is on the loose. And that reminds me, your skinny assistant was down at the station again nosing around. What's up with that?"

Dana didn't answer right away. She wanted to choose her words carefully and avoid an argument. "She's doing a background piece on the Royal Flush murders. Nothing that will step on your toes," she added quickly.

"I'll bet," Bruno said sarcastically. "Come on, give with the details."

"I don't know the details. She just asked if she could do a background story on the street people and their plight. One of the victims was an old man who hung around her mother's neighborhood."

At that moment, Lucille arrived with their lunch orders. Dana gave her a big smile. "Thanks, Lucille. This looks heavenly."

Bruno nodded and stopped asking questions and concentrated on the heaping plate of food in front of him.

"I hope you're going to have a small salad for dinner tonight," Dana commented.

"I'm sure I won't get dinner," Bruno complained. "Once I report in, I'll be too busy trying to track down Peter Hogan and the serial killer."

"Okay," Dana said firmly. "Let's forget about our jobs for a moment and just enjoy our lunch."

They ate in silence for a few minutes. Dana was savoring every bite of the juicy hamburger and crisp deep-fried onion rings. Bruno seemed similarly enthralled with his meal.

"There's an art exhibit at Del's Gallery on Sunday afternoon," Dana finally said. "I'm going. Do you want to tag along?"

"Only if I can hang around the buffet table and not talk to anyone with purple hair."

"Are you off duty on Sunday?"

"I don't know yet. It depends on how far we get on the two homicide cases."

"Right," Dana replied thoughtfully. She also had

two homicides to work on now. The tape recorder, the tape, and the fact that Peter Hogan was probably trying to blackmail Charles Wright convinced her that both murders were connected. If both murders were connected and Peter Hogan wasn't a killer, that left two other suspects. Charles Wright and Paulette Mason.

"What are you daydreaming about?" Bruno asked.

"I was thinking about Charles Wright," she replied honestly. "Do you think he's capable of murder?"

"Given the right motivation."

"And the possibility of seeing his hopes and dreams crash and burn might be enough to motivate him, don't you agree?"

"I agree with that, but I don't think he would take the chance. The taped interview wasn't that damaging. It made the wife look like a shrew—probably get the guy more votes if it were made public. Besides, even if he iced his wife, how would he have gotten to the old gal in the retirement home?"

"I don't know, but if Hogan was trying to blackmail him, Wright may have been convinced there was something more on the tape, something that would cost him the election. Maybe Madeline told him that there was something on it just to taunt him. So he murders Leona to silence her, then drags Madeline to Hogan's apartment intending to kill them both. Maybe Hogan is dead too, but Wright got rid of the body so everyone would think that Hogan killed Madeline."

"And left the tape and recorder behind for the police to find and trace back to him?"

"Yes," Dana said, warming up to her new theory. "Once he discovered there was nothing vital on the tape, he had no reason to try and dispose of it. He left it, along with the blackmail evidence, to make things look worse for Peter."

"Now, it's Peter," Bruno said sharply. "I didn't think you knew him that well."

"I'm just talking, Bruno, trying to work out a theory."

"Sorry, sweets. I don't think it holds water. The idea of a prominent guy like Wright sneaking around a retirement home in the middle of the night to kill an old lady is ridiculous. Your friend, Peter, is the perp. Case closed."

"Not until you catch him," Dana replied, stubbornly. "The case isn't closed until someone locates Peter Hogan and finds out what really happened to Leona and Madeline."

Bruno sighed and sat back against the flowered fabric that lined the booth. "He's a killer, Dana. You track him down, and you call me or another cop, understand? I don't want you near that guy alone."

Dana smiled. "Why, thank you."

"For what?"

"For thinking that I can track down Hogan before the police do."

"That's one of the problems between us," Bruno said quietly. "You get involved in a case and you don't stop. You're just too clever for your own good, and it worries the hell out of me."

Dana reached across the table and patted his hand. "I'll be careful," she promised.

Bruno grabbed her hand and held on tight. "And you'll call me if you get a lead on Hogan?"

"Wow, look at the time," Dana said, brightly. "I've got to get to the office. I'll pay the check, you leave the tip."

TWENTY

WHEN DANA ARRIVED at her office, Marianne handed her a stack of phone messages. One of them was from Erna. Dana quickly dialed the number, which was probably her home phone. Erna answered on the second ring.

"I talked to Peter," Erna said after Dana identified herself.

"When?"

"Early this morning. I didn't know if you were coming back to Peaceful Pines, so I called the number on your card. You have a secretary and everything—you must be an important investigator."

"I just work for an important newspaper," Dana replied. "So tell me about Peter."

"He swears he did not kill anyone. I told him you wanted to help him. He said he would contact you."

"When?"

"I don't know. I gave him all the numbers on your card. He is very frightened. He needs your help. I told him you would not turn him over to the police. That is true, isn't it?"

"Yes," Dana told her. "Did he give you any indication of where he is?"

"No. He hung up quickly after I gave him your numbers."

"Thank you, Erna. I guess all I can do now is wait for him to contact me."

"You are welcome as long as you do not hurt Peter. He is a good boy. I know he did not hurt Leona or that fancy woman."

"Right," Dana agreed. "One more thing. Do you know anything about Mr. Templeton acting inappropriately with the female workers?"

Erna laughed out loud. "He is a creepy man. The girls run when they see him coming."

"Why do they run?" Dana persisted.

"I don't know. I just know they do not like to be near him."

"Look, Erna, can you give me the names of any of the girls who run from Templeton? I need to talk to them."

"They are mostly girls on the day shift. I do not know them well. I just hear things."

"Look, I'll be back to work tonight. In the meantime, can you try and get some names for me? There are a lot of women working there and I don't have time to talk to them all."

"You are coming back to work tonight?"

"Yes. Can you get some names for me?"

"I will try," Erna promised. "I will ask Judy, my friend who works on days."

The phone call ended, and Dana sat back in her chair and swiveled it around to look out the window.

The wind was blowing, sending swirls of dust and small particles of paper dancing through the air.

She had the names of the women Milecki had questioned and would talk to them. If Erna could find more women who might have a valid reason to complain about Templeton, she would be justified in digging deeper into the director's past. Men who tried to take advantage of the women who worked for them usually had a history that could be verified.

Dana sighed and turned back to her desk and the stack of mail and other messages that needed her attention. The rest of the afternoon passed quickly, but at the end of the day Dana felt like she had made progress in sorting through the problems and making notes as to how they were to be handled.

Marianne came in and took the pile that could be answered by letter. Some of the problems only required research. Marianne was an expert on finding consumer groups who would help with disreputable repairmen, or organizations who offered assistance to people who needed legal help or advice.

"Is it okay if I leave a little early?" Marianne asked.

"Sure," Dana replied. "I'm sure I owe you lots of time. You're always staying late to help me out."

"Bob talked me into going out with his brother-in-law," Marianne said in a rush. "I hope this doesn't turn into a disaster. Dating a relative of someone you work with isn't a good policy."

Dana smiled. "So he finally wore you down. Well,

I'm sure it will be fun. Bob will make certain you're both properly entertained, even if you hate each other."

"Oh, God," Marianne exclaimed. "Do you think we will? Hate each other, that is? Have you met his brother-in-law?"

"Of course not," Dana said quickly. "I was just joking. Don't tell me that you, who have men falling over their own feet to get a look at you, are worried about a blind date."

"Thank you for the ego boost," Marianne said. "But lately, the guys I've dated have only been interested in getting me into bed. I'd like to build a relationship around more than sex. You know, I'd like what you and Bruno have."

Dana laughed and shook her head. "As the saying goes, be careful what you wish for, you might get it."

"Come on, Dana," Marianne insisted. "Bruno adores you."

"Sometimes," Dana replied. "Sometimes not. Anyway, I'm sure Bob's brother-in-law is a very nice guy. I can't wait until tomorrow to hear all about it."

"Right," Marianne said. "I will give you a full report in the morning."

They both laughed at that. The phone rang, and Marianne picked it up. "Okay, thanks. I'll tell her," she said.

Hanging up the phone, Marianne hurried across

the room and flipped on the television that stood on a credenza against the far wall.

"That was Casey. Charles Wright is holding a press conference. She thought you'd want to see it."

Dana got up and walked closer to the television. She and Marianne watched in rapt attention as the candidate's handsome face filled the screen.

"That's a fair question," Wright said to someone offscreen. "Unfortunately, this is a police investigation, and I'm not at liberty to share that information at this time."

"Are you a suspect in your wife's murder?" a voice off camera called out.

"I was questioned at length yesterday and again today. As you can see, I am not in custody, nor do I expect to be questioned again."

"Is it going to be business as usual for your campaign?" another voice asked.

"Obviously, my wife's death has changed my life dramatically. It's going to be very difficult to carry on, but Madeline was my strongest supporter. She would want me to continue, and therefore I will continue. The campaign will only be put on hold for a few days."

Someone asked about funeral arrangements, but Wright declined to answer saying the services would be private. Then, Paulette took over. She thanked everyone while Charles made a quick exit, and the press conference ended.

AN HOUR LATER, Paulette and Charles were in the den of his luxurious home sipping cocktails in front of a roaring fire. They occupied opposite ends of a long, brocaded sofa.

"I think the press conference went quite well," Paulette said.

"I hope so. After all the time and money that's been invested in this campaign the last thing I want is to have it damaged by circumstances beyond our control."

Paulette looked at him over the rim of her glass. "Your wife was murdered. That will evoke a certain amount of sympathy from the voters as you bravely carry on without her."

"What about that tape the police have?"

"What about it? There was nothing significant on it."

"No, but if it's made public, the very fact that she said unflattering things about me could hurt my image. Damn her, and damn that nosy old woman. May they both rot in hell."

Paulette moved closer and placed her hand on his arm. "The one I'm worried about is Peter Hogan. Obviously, Madeline was working with him. When the police find him, he's going to try to blame you for her death."

"We'll just have to hope that he never gets a chance to talk to the police."

Paulette backed away. "Is it possible that Madeline gave him other information that we have to worry about?"

"Of course not. Madeline didn't know that much. I'm just concerned about the campaign and hope that the cops never find him. As long as he's a fugitive, he's the most likely suspect in Madeline's death. I shouldn't have to explain this to you, Paulette." His tone was sharp.

Angered by his remark, Paulette got up and walked over to the fireplace. "I don't like your tone, Charles."

"I'm sorry. I'm upset."

"As much as I disliked her, I didn't want to see harm come to Madeline," Paulette told him evenly. "I hope you know that, Charles."

"Yes. I know that."

"Of course you do." She looked contrite. "It's just that this whole thing is so upsetting. The campaign was moving along so well. Even when Madeline came back from Florida so unexpectedly, I thought we would be able to handle her. Now that's she gone and gotten herself killed, it's a different story. Wherever you go there will be questions to answer." She paused and thought about it for a moment. "You'll just have to take the same position you voiced today. No comment on an ongoing police investigation."

"Yes, darling," he said patiently. "That is what we decided earlier."

"Don't look at me like that. I'm not falling apart. I'm just a bit unnerved."

Charles rose from the sofa. Joining her at the fireplace he put his arms around her and laughed softly. "Perhaps we should both just be grateful that Madeline is no longer a problem."

Paulette nodded. "Madeline was a conniving witch."

"A lot like you, my darling. The difference is that you have chosen to use your talents to help me win an election."

Paulette started to protest, but Charles pulled her closer and stopped her words with a passionate kiss. He released her just as suddenly and walked back to the sofa and sat down again.

Paulette looked at him for a long time before she spoke again. "Even if the old woman's tape isn't that damaging, there's no telling what Madeline may have told Hogan personally. Apparently he thought he had enough derogatory information that you would pay him to keep quiet. The police already know that he was attempting to extort money from you." Paulette finished her little speech and waited for Charles to comment on the facts she had just presented.

"I told you, Madeline didn't really know anything that could hurt us. But you're right, if Hogan is arrested, it will be his word against mine. Who do you think people will believe?"

Paulette looked directly into his eyes with a hint of a smile playing around the corners of her brightly colored lips. Charles' kiss had not managed to smear any of the makeup she applied so carefully each morning. Now as she debated how to answer his question, she still looked like a perfectly painted porcelain doll.

"Well?" Charles prompted again. "Who do you think the voters will believe, me or Peter Hogan?"

Paulette returned to the sofa and kissed him lightly on the face. "Your word is golden, Charles, like your looks and reputation. So let's concentrate on more important matters. I think you should go to Chicago again. That's where the majority of the votes will come from."

IT WAS one of Dr. Mary's nights to see patients, and Dana helped the elderly doctor set up shop. When they were ready, Dana opened the office door to admit the first resident and was surprised to see Rocky standing at the head of the line. He smiled at Dana and walked quickly past her to sit down in the chair next to Dr. Mary.

"Do you have a problem, Rocky?" Dr. Mary asked pointedly.

"Yes. I apologize."

"You don't look sorry."

"That's only because my face is stubborn. It refuses to show what is in my heart."

"Well, let me see if you are telling the truth." Dr. Mary took his arm and began to wrap her blood pressure band around it.

Rocky sat silently while she pumped the gauge and read his blood pressure. Dana watched as Dr. Mary nodded and removed the band from his arm.

"What does it say?" Rocky asked.

"It is normal," she replied, popping a thermometer into his open mouth and taking his pulse.

Puzzled, Dana turned to the next person in line who was Mrs. Sobitsky.

"What's going on?" Dana asked softly.

"Rocky said Dr. Mary was a quack and he would never let her touch him. He said it at breakfast this morning and she got very upset and has not talked to him since."

"Why would he say a thing like that?" Dana whispered.

"Because he was jealous," Mrs. Sobitsky whispered back. "We got a new man in this morning and he was putting the moves on Dr. Mary."

Dana couldn't hide her amusement and Mrs. Sobitsky wagged a finger at her. "You young people think you are the only ones who can fall in love, but there is plenty of romance in this place."

"Really." Dana wanted to get more of this story, but Erna called out to her from the end of the corridor.

"Excuse me," Dana told Mrs. Sobitsky.

"I see Rocky and Dr. Mary are making up," Erna said when Dana joined her. "I heard that Rocky was very mean to her this morning."

"Mrs. Sobitsky said he was jealous. She also said there is plenty of romance here," Dana told her.

Erna nodded. "We keep the men and women on separate floors, but there is an elevator." She smiled. "Of course there are more women than men here, so

Mr. Tishner will have no trouble finding someone else to charm."

"I take it Mr. Tishner is the new man who tried to put the moves on Dr. Mary?" Dana asked.

Erna laughed. "You see why I love these old people."

"I'm becoming quite fond of them myself," Dana admitted.

Rocky came out of the reception office looking very pleased with himself. "Dr. Mary is an excellent physician," he announced to the others who were standing patiently in the line. "She will take good care of you."

His mission apparently accomplished, Rocky took a seat in the lobby to wait for Dr. Mary to finish her office hours. Dana turned back to Erna.

"Did you get some names for me?" she asked.

"Here is the list of names and phone numbers. Call after three o'clock in the afternoon. That is when their shifts end."

Dana took the folded paper that Erna held out to her. The telephone rang, and Dana hurried back to the reception office to answer it. Erna went back down the corridor to her own office.

As Dr. Mary continued to see her patients, Dana studied the list that Erna had provided. There were four names on it. She would call each woman tomorrow and see if Milecki's theory about John Templeton held any validity.

TWENTY-ONE

MARIANNE LET GREG TUCK her hand into the crook of his arm as they left the theater. Bob and Cynthia were walking a little ahead of them. Bob stopped a few feet from the theater exit and waited for them to catch up. "You guys want to get some coffee?" Bob asked. "I know an all-night café that has fabulous homemade pie."

Cynthia rolled her eyes. "Bob, you're supposed to be on a diet."

"So, he can just have coffee," Greg told his sister.

"Come on, honey," Bob said quickly. "One piece of pie won't hurt."

Cynthia was a dark-haired, dark-eyed girl with a solid athletic body and a wholesome face. She and Bob were an unlikely-looking pair, but their personalities balanced each other very well. They had been married for six years and had two boisterous sons.

"Come on, sis," Greg prodded. "You fixed me up with this incredibly beautiful girl and I don't want the evening cut short."

Marianne smiled up at Greg. He was tall and broad shouldered. Dark hair and eyes seemed to be a family trait and were further enhanced by Greg's winning smile and easygoing manner. He wasn't as good-looking as most of the men she dated, but he was charming and considerate, and Marianne had thoroughly enjoyed their evening together.

"It's after twelve," Cynthia said. "What about the babysitter?"

"I told her we'd be out late. She brought her pillow and blanket so she could sack out on the sofa." Bob turned to Marianne. "What do you say, Marianne?" Bob asked.

"I could use a cup of coffee," she replied.

Bob gave Marianne his most brilliant "I told you so" smile. "Great. Let's go." He took his wife's arm and headed toward the car.

They had all driven together in Bob's car. It was parked in the lot next door to the theater. Marianne and Greg got into the back seat. Bob drove out of the lot and turned into an alley.

"Where are you going?" Cynthia asked.

"It angles over to Fourth Street where the café is," Bob said. "It's the quickest route to a big slice of hot apple pie."

Cynthia groaned at her husband's obvious hurry to reach the high-calorie dessert he craved, and she began a discourse on the wisdom of Bob ordering something like a bowl of fresh fruit or low fat yogurt. Her words were cut short as Bob maneuvered the car around the bend of the alley and the headlight shone on a frightening scene.

A shabby looking man was down on his knees in

the alley. A dark cloaked figure was standing over him, but took off running as the headlights illuminated the scene. Cynthia screamed and Bob slammed on the brakes to avoid running over the man who had now collapsed on the pavement.

"Call the police," Bob shouted as he jumped out of the car and ran after the person dressed in black. Greg tried to open the back door of the car, but Bob had engaged the childproof locks and he couldn't open them from the back seat. He reached over Marianne and the back seat and disengaged it. Once he got the door open he took off after Bob.

Cynthia was yelling for them to come back. Marianne retrieved her cell phone from her purse, punched in nine-one-one and reported the crime they had come upon to the emergency dispatcher. Within seconds, the sound of sirens could be heard.

Marianne got out of the car and looked at the man sprawled out in the alley. He was flat on his back with a knife protruding from his chest. His ragged clothes were soaked with blood. With the headlights still lighting up the scene, Marianne didn't have to touch the victim to see that he was dead and that the killer had once again left his signature. The playing cards were scattered around the body as if the killer had flung them down in haste before running away.

A few seconds later, Bob and Greg returned. Bob was breathing hard, trying to catch his breath. He was unable to speak. They carefully skirted the murder scene.

Greg, who was in much better shape than Bob, told Marianne that the killer had too great a lead on him and had disappeared into the darkness of the next street.

"That's it," Bob said, still gasping for air. "Tomorrow I go on a real diet."

"I might have been able to catch him, if I hadn't been trapped in the back seat with those childproof locks," Greg told him. "He must have had a car nearby. I heard an engine start up, but by the time I got to the corner, it was gone."

"You're both crazy," Cynthia shouted from the car. "You could have been killed."

Greg looked at Marianne and shrugged. Bob hurried back to the car to calm his wife down.

"Your sister is right," Marianne told Greg. "You don't know if the man you were chasing had another weapon. Some of his victims have been shot to death. He probably had a gun."

Greg smiled at her. "Were you really worried about me?"

"I was terrified," Marianne said with a catch in her voice.

"I'm sorry," Greg said. He moved forward and put his arms around her. "I used to be a cop, and I guess the old instincts just took over."

Marianne let him gather her against him. Now

that the crisis had passed, she was trembling. "You were a cop?"

"In Chicago."

"I thought you were a social worker."

"I am now. I decided that I would be happier counseling kids and trying to keep them out of trouble instead of arresting them after they got into trouble."

Marianne nodded and leaned against him, liking the solid feel of his chest and the strength of his arms holding her.

A few seconds later, an ambulance and a squad car arrived on the scene.

Marianne and Greg's first date ended at the police station where they all gave accounts of the murder scene they had happened upon to a police stenographer.

IN A DARK APARTMENT on the outskirts of Crescent Hills, the Royal Flush killer was contemplating the night's close call. The headlights had been startling, the chase even more unexpected.

Hopefully the victim was dead and would be unable to provide the police with any information. The people who pursued the killer did not get close enough to give more than a general description of height, weight, and clothing, so they posed no real threat.

The killer was reasonably sure they had not even seen the car parked on the next street. Slow, out-of-shape men who could not catch a snail. No, the men tonight posed no threat to the mission, but there were others who did.

"I will have to stop the killings here," the killer said softly. "It's time to move on. I will take care of the loose ends and slip away."

This was the first time that there had been any loose ends to hinder the mission, and they would be the last. In the next town the killer would change the routine. There were many ways to leave the message and thinking of something new, something more appropriate, was now in order.

But first the loose ends.

Rising from the sofa in the sparsely furnished living room, the killer moved quietly to the bedroom. The chase and the possibility of capture had caused the adrenaline to flow and the physical effects lingered making each movement effortless and smooth.

A weapon had been lost tonight, but it was of no consequence, a standard knife obtained in another time, another place. It was one of many, and was untraceable.

Settling into bed, the mind and body continued to race. It was time to move on, but the departure could not be too sudden. In other towns, there had been regrets, parties to wish the killer well. There would not be any of that here.

Learn a lesson from this, the killer thought. You have chosen your mission and performed it well.

One small slip had led to complications, and the mission had been jeopardized. That could never happen again.

TWENTY-TWO

THE NEXT MORNING, at the staff meeting in Dana's office, Bob and Marianne recounted the events of the night before. Casey was obviously miffed.

"Damn," she said. "I wish I would have been there."

"With those long legs of yours, you could have caught the guy and gotten the rest of the deck," Bob told her.

"Cut it out, Bob," Marianne warned. "You and Greg had no business running down a dark alley after that maniac."

Dana looked at her secretary. "Not a great ending to your first date."

"Are you going to give the guy another chance?" Casey asked.

Marianne smiled and looked over at Bob.

"Oh, admit you like him," Bob said. "You can still keep the twenty bucks."

"Twenty bucks?" Casey shouted. "You only offered me ten to go out with him."

"You said you wouldn't go out with one of my relatives for a thousand," Bob countered.

"You mean I was second choice?" Marianne asked.

"Listen," Bob replied. "Greg's been really lonely since he moved here and I was just trying to connect him with someone I liked."

"I'll tell you what, Casey," Marianne said. "I'll use Bob's twenty to take you to lunch today. Greg's really a great guy and I'm glad you didn't get to him first."

Bob got up and did a little victory dance, and Dana threw a memo pad at him. "Excuse me," she said, through her laughter. "While I find this episode of the dating game fascinating, we have some business-related issues to discuss this morning."

Everyone settled down. They went over the pending cases that Casey and Bob were working on and Dana brought them up to date on her investigation at Peaceful Pines.

"Leona's murder seems to be connected to the murder of Madeline Wright, especially if you accept Peter Hogan as a killer."

"But you don't believe he's guilty, do you?" Casey said.

"No. I think he teamed up with Madeline Wright to blackmail her husband, but from my personal contact with him and the information other people at Peaceful Pines have given me, I don't buy him as the killer."

"What does Bruno think?" Casey asked.

"Bruno is ready to pin every murder in town on the guy," Dana replied.

"That would be convenient," Bob said. "But we saw the Royal Flush killer, and from his general description, Hogan is too tall. The killer was shorter. Isn't that right, Marianne?"

Marianne nodded her affirmation to his statement.

"Dana, have you had time to look at the report I made up on the case?" Casey asked.

"Yes. And I think that if the police did as much research as you did, they might have caught the killer by now."

"I won't tell Bruno you said that," Marianne said.

"Do you think I should talk to the police about my theory on the playing cards before we run the article?" Casey asked.

"What theory?" Bob asked.

Casey looked at Dana, who nodded for her to explain.

"The cards found on the first four victims came from the same deck of cards. The fifth victim was found with a Diamond flush, new deck but the same type of playing cards. But then the killer switched to a new deck of cards from a different manufacturer."

"So the question is why didn't the killer continue to use the cards from the second deck?" Marianne asked.

"Right. I think something happened to the second

deck. The killer lost them somehow and had to start another new deck."

"Okay, that makes sense," Bob said. "So what's your theory?"

"I found out that the manufacturer of the lost deck doesn't sell to retail outlets. Their cards are part of a gaming package that is sold to recreational facilities along with checkers, dominoes, and other such games." Casey paused to let this information sink in. Bob and Marianne nodded for her to continue. "The police are not actively looking for the lost deck. Instead they are checking all the outlets in the area that sell the new cards the killer is using now. They are hoping someone will remember selling the cards to the killer during the time between the fifth and sixth murders."

"Sounds like standard procedure to me," Bob remarked.

"Except," Casey replied, her voice rising with excitement, "hundreds of people buy these decks of playing cards, but only one person could have the deck with the missing Diamonds. Find the lost deck of cards and it may lead to the killer."

"What if the killer still has the deck and just decided to stop using it?" Marianne asked.

"Then the article we are going to run in the evening edition won't do much good," Dana replied. "However, Sam thinks it's worth a try. We're going to ask anyone who may have found an incomplete deck of cards during that same time period to contact the police."

"Everyone admits that the cards are a vital link to the killer. Find the lost deck and it may lead back to the killer," Bob said. "It's a lot easier than trying to chase the guy down a dark alley."

The meeting ended and Dana turned her thoughts to Charles Wright. Spouses were always the prime suspects in a homicide case like Madeline Wright's. Just because Wright had been released didn't mean that the police had ruled him out.

Although Bruno had said that the tape in Hogan's apartment didn't contain anything that would really damage Wright's image, Dana's instincts told her there had to be more.

Hogan didn't strike her as unintelligent. He would not have stolen Leona's tape and attempted to blackmail Wright if there was no flame to be fanned. Even a tiny spark of scandal had the potential of erupting into a blazing inferno for a man in the public eye. The news media was always looking for a hint of impropriety involving a high-profile figure.

Dana was betting there was another tape, one that contained information that Wright would do anything to keep secret. The tape found in Hogan's apartment may have been only a teaser used to get Wright's attention.

Perhaps a trip to Florida to the resort where Madeline Wright spent so much time would turn up a lead. She had to have talked to people there, maybe confided in someone. People who were far from home often felt safe telling their tales to new acquaintances. Dana was reasonably sure the Crescent Hills police would eventually dispatch someone there in connection with the investigation.

The problem was that Crescent Hills didn't have the manpower found in larger cities like Chicago, and the Royal Flush murders had all of the personnel pulling double duty.

Dana smiled at the idea of escaping the cold and rain for a dose of warmth and sunshine even for a few days. She would actually be doing a service for the police department by going to Florida and trying to uncover new evidence in the Wright homicide case. Sam would probably approve the expenditure, since it was most definitely connected to Leona's murder.

Marianne buzzed in with a call, ending Dana's daydream of white sand and foamy surf. It was Bruno calling to invite Dana to lunch.

They met at Big Lou's and Dana kept the conversation light, telling him about the romantic relationship that was developing between Rocky and Dr. Mary.

"He said something that really reminded me of you," Dana said.

"Good or bad?" Bruno asked.

"He said that his face was too stubborn to show what was in his heart."

"You think I have a stubborn face?"

"Definitely. Of course, being a cop, I guess you'd

have to have a stubborn face. Can't let suspects know that underneath that scowl is a soft heart."

Bruno grunted. "You're the only one my heart gets mushy over."

"Thank you," Dana replied.

"So how's your investigation going?" Bruno asked, changing the subject. "You ready to give up the bogus job at Peaceful Pines?"

"I don't know. Erna gave me the names of some women who work on the day shift. They may shed some light on Milecki's theory about Templeton."

"You're wasting your time, sweets. Hogan is the perp. He's got motive and opportunity."

"What about Charles Wright?"

"No physical evidence to tie him to either crime. He cooperated fully and we had no reason to hold him."

"Are you sending someone to Florida to check out people that Madeline Wright may have talked to there?" Dana asked, keeping her tone casual.

"We might." Bruno looked at her suspiciously. "I suppose you've already made a plane reservation?"

Dana laughed. "Not yet. I was just thinking that if Hogan was attempting to blackmail Wright, there had to be more to it. Unless you weren't totally honest with me about what was on that tape you confiscated."

"You're a reporter. I'm only totally honest with you when it comes to our personal relationship."

"Then there was more on the tape?"

"No."

Dana didn't know whether to believe him or not, but decided not to pursue the subject because the waitress arrived with their lunch order. She delivered a bacon, lettuce, and tomato club sandwich with a mound of french fries to Bruno and a chef's salad to Dana.

They ate in silence for a few minutes. Then Bruno asked what Bob and Marianne had told Dana about stumbling on the murder scene the night before.

"Bob swears he's going on a diet. Said if he wasn't so out of shape, he could have caught the killer," Dana said.

"Greg is an ex-cop, you know," Bruno said as he dumped ketchup over his fries. "If he hadn't been trapped in the back seat with Marianne, he might have been able to nab the guy."

"So I was told. Marianne liked him. I think Bob may have engineered a successful blind date." She reached over and snitched a french fry from Bruno's plate. "Any new clues turn up from what they witnessed or the murder scene itself?"

"No comment," Bruno replied.

"Casey came up with a very interesting idea," Dana said slowly. "Do you want to hear it?"

"No."

"Okay," Dana told him cheerfully. "I'll shut up. No need to start the lecture."

"Like lecturing you would stop you from...oh, hell. Is this interesting idea going to be in your afternoon edition?"

"Yes."

Bruno's dark eyes clouded and Dana braced herself for the verbal storm that was sure to follow. The argument was avoided by another interruption. This time it was Bruno's pager. He yanked it off his belt and read the display.

"I have to get back to the station. We'll talk about this later," Bruno said. He picked up his half-eaten lunch and carried it to the counter where Big Lou put it in a take-out container and promised to put the lunches on his tab.

He was out the door in a matter of minutes. Dana sighed and stuck her fork into a cherry tomato. "Can't say I didn't try to warn him," she whispered to herself.

TWENTY-THREE

DANA RETURNED to her office to find Sam McGowan waiting for her. "Helen has been moved from Intensive Care to a regular room. I thought we could try to talk to her again."

"Good idea," Dana said. "I have some new questions to ask."

On the way to the hospital, Dana told Sam about the suspicions that had surfaced about Templeton.

"I classified him as a sleazebag the first time he gave me one of his oily smiles," Sam said.

At the hospital, Helen was looking much better. Some color had returned to her cheeks and she was sitting up in bed. Unfortunately, she was still not able to speak and her diminished motor skills made it impossible for her to communicate in writing.

Dana slowly voiced her questions about Templeton and his behavior toward the female employees. Helen just seemed confused by the questions and after a few frustrating minutes rang the call button for the nurse again.

"I don't think she can remember anything," Dana told Sam on the drive back to the paper.

"I agree," Sam said. "From what I know about

strokes, they can impair your short-term memory. Actually, every time we see her she sends us away sooner. I think our visits are upsetting her. Although she may not understand why that's so."

"Maybe I'll have better luck talking to the women that Erna told me about. By the way, Erna has been in touch with Peter Hogan and told him we want to help him."

"Don't try to deal with him on your own," Sam warned.

"He didn't kill Leona," Dana said. "Dr. Mary ruled him out as a suspect there."

"But he may have killed Madeline Wright," Sam insisted.

"Now you sound like Bruno."

"As much as I want to find Leona's killer, I don't want to put you in danger in the process. You do understand that?"

"Of course I do," Dana replied. "Don't worry, I have no intention of doing anything foolish if I can help it." Sam shot her a stern look and she smiled at him. "I'll be careful."

Sam parked the car in *The Globe* lot and listened to Dana's thoughts about Charles Wright.

"What does Bruno think about extending the investigation to Florida?"

"He said they might send someone there, but to tell you the truth, they are so tied up with the Royal Flush murders, I don't think it will be anytime soon."

"It may be worth a try," Sam said. "Especially if Hogan doesn't turn up."

Sam left Dana with the promise that he would have his secretary check with his travel agent about the flights to Florida.

At three-fifteen, Dana instructed Marianne to hold all her calls and keep any visitors at a distance while she called the women on Erna's list.

There were four names on the list. Two of them denied any knowledge of inappropriate behavior by Templeton. The other two supplied information that gave Dana a whole new perspective on Leona's murder.

"Templeton let every woman on the day shift know he was looking for some action, until the day that Leona marched into his office and told him off. We all got a good laugh out of Leona putting him in his place. Now the only one he talks to is his girlfriend, Hatterly," a nurse's aide named Betty told Dana. "I guess since he's focusing all his attention on her, they've gotten pretty hot and heavy these days. She even changed to the evening shift, so they could sneak off to an empty room after lights out for the residents."

Betty's story was confirmed by Erna's friend, Judy. "I'm surprised Erna didn't tell you. She walked in on them once."

"Well," Dana replied. "I asked Erna about the possibility of sexual harassment. If Mrs. Hatterly is a willing participant in the affair, it's not harassment."

"I guess not." Judy laughed.

"What did Mrs. Hatterly think about Leona's confrontation of Templeton?"

"She was mad as hell, but she didn't say anything to her. I guess she didn't want Leona to get on her case too."

"Did Leona know about the affair between Templeton and Hatterly?"

"Oh, sure. Leona knew everything that went on. She was an amazing person, so quick and clever. I really miss her."

"One more question," Dana said. "Do you think that Mrs. Hatterly could have felt threatened by Leona?"

Judy thought about it for a few seconds before answering. "Well, I suppose she could have been worried that Leona would cause trouble for her. She and Templeton are both married to other people, you know."

Dana hung up the phone and turned her chair around and gazed out the window. The view from her window wasn't anything special, mostly other buildings in the downtown area, but it gave her something unimportant to focus on when she was in her thinking mode.

A cold misty rain spattered the window, obstructing her view, but not her concentration. The weather forecast predicted that the rain would turn into snow before the day ended.

After the first evening when Templeton had showed

her around Peaceful Pines and introduced her to the staff, the director had never hung around during her shift. Neither had Mrs. Hatterly ventured from her domain on the second floor. It hadn't occurred to Dana before, but they were both making a point of avoiding any type of contact with her. She wondered if her presence at Peaceful Pines was putting a strain on their romantic relationship. Obviously, an illicit affair was something they would want to hide.

Hatterly and Templeton were both aware of Leona's close friendship with Sam McGowan, the editor of an influential newspaper. The question was how far would they go to keep their affair from becoming a public scandal.

Dana spun around and opened a desk drawer. She withdrew the file folder with Milecki's reports and looked for an interview with Nurse Hatterly. There was none.

She picked up the phone and called Sergeant Milecki. He came on the line, chuckling. "Did you decide to dump the brute and give me a chance?" he said.

"What would your wife say about that?" Dana countered.

"She'd be glad to share the burden with someone else."

Dana laughed. "Sorry, I can't help her out. Listen, I have a quick question for you on the Rosetti case."

"Shoot."

"I don't see an interview report with the other head

nurse who works the evening shift at Peaceful Pines, a Mrs. Hatterly. Did anyone talk to her?"

"If it's not in there, we didn't interview her. I think the murder happened on her night off. Pretty much ruled her out as a suspect. Why? You on to something?"

"I don't know," Dana answered honestly. "I'll call you when I know more."

"I'll look forward to it," Milecki said.

TWENTY-FOUR

DANA WAITED until all the residents were in the dining room before she called Erna and asked her to come to the reception office.

They had spoken only briefly earlier when Erna had introduced her to a middle-aged man named Harry, who had been hired to take Peter Hogan's place on the evening shift.

"How's Harry working out?" Dana asked when Erna came into the office.

"He's a nice man. The old ladies are already buttering him up with compliments. I sent him to the dining room to help out during supper."

"Have you heard anything else from Peter?"

Erna shook her head. "Did you talk to Judy and the others today?"

"Yes," Dana said. "They told me that Mrs. Hatterly and John Templeton are having an affair."

Erna shrugged. "That is old news."

"It could be important if Hatterly or Templeton were worried about Leona exposing their affair."

Erna shook her head again. "To who? Everyone already knows."

"What about their respective spouses? What about the Board of Directors of Peaceful Pines?"

Erna's mouth opened and she took a step back. "Oh...I did not think of that. The Board of Directors meet here every month. Leona died just two days before the meeting."

"Would Leona have had an opportunity to talk to any of the board members?"

"Sure. They walk around, talk to the residents. Ask them questions. Many of the residents are confused and talk nonsense. No one would pay attention to them, but Leona was different. They would listen to her."

The telephone buzzed and Dana answered it. "It's for you, Erna. Something about a linen order."

"I must go back to my office. I'll talk to you later, Dana."

"Right. Thanks for all your help, Erna. I really appreciate it."

Dana sat down and contemplated their conversation. She now had two new suspects in the murder of Leona Rosetti. Either of them could have acted alone, or they could have pulled it off together. First thing tomorrow she would discuss the probabilities with Sam. Ordinarily, she would call Bruno and talk to him, but he probably wouldn't be speaking to her after he saw the article in *The Globe*'s afternoon edition.

Casey's article was going to cause a big problem for them. Dana had intended to warn Bruno at lunch, trying to diffuse some of his anger before it ignited. Because the article was written by a member of Dana's staff, Bruno would blame her. Her one hope was that the article would result in a tangible lead to the serial killer. If that happened, Bruno would have to back down and admit that Casey's research was valuable.

A kitchen worker delivered Dana's supper and she ate it absently, hardly tasting the watery beef concoction spooned over noodles. Dessert was two chocolate chip cookies. Dana wrapped them in a napkin and put them in her purse for later.

The rest of the evening passed slowly. Rocky and Dr. Mary stopped by to chat. They seemed to be very content with each other this evening and didn't linger in the lobby very long.

Dana wanted to ask them about Mrs. Hatterly and Templeton, but thought better of it. First she would find out if her new suspects had solid alibis for the night Leona died. Templeton's interview report said that he was home with his wife on the night in question, but no one had verified that with his wife. That would have to be done, and Mrs. Hatterly would have to be interviewed by the police as well. Given Dana's newly formed friendship with Sergeant Milecki maybe that wouldn't pose a problem. Dana could call the Sergeant and give him the information she had uncovered and let him take it from there.

Finally it was time to close up the office. Dana

went down the hall to Erna's office to say good night.

"Tomorrow is my day off," Erna told her. "I was thinking I should go to the hospital and see Helen. I hear she is doing better."

"Yes. They moved her to a regular room."

"Then you've talked to her again?"

"Not really," Dana said. "She's very confused. Whenever we try to talk to her, she rings for the nurse and we get sent away."

"Confusion is very common in stroke patients," Erna said.

Outside the temperature had dropped below freezing, but the snow that had been forecast had not yet materialized.

Her car was parked at the end of the row in the employee parking area near the woods that surrounded the retirement home. As Dana approached her car she could see that the windows were beginning to frost over.

Using her gloved hand, Dana swiped at the frost that was forming on the windshield. A security car passed by and stopped to look at her. She waved at the driver, and he continued on by.

A moment later, Dana unlocked the car, but before she had time to get inside, a strong arm grabbed her from behind and a hand was clamped across her mouth.

A voice spoke softly in her ear. "It's Peter. I have to talk to you. Get in the car and get us out of here."

TWENTY-FIVE

DANA'S HEART WAS SLAMMING against her ribs. Peter took his hand away from her face and she let loose with a number of colorful expletives.

"Sorry. I didn't mean to scare you," Peter said as they both scrambled into the car. He ducked down in the back seat and Dana slid behind the steering wheel in the front. She took a deep breath and started the engine.

Neither of them spoke again until they were safely past the gate and out on the highway.

"You can get up now," Dana said.

Peter struggled to an upright position on the back seat. "Where are we going?"

"To my apartment where I can record your statement."

"I didn't kill anybody."

"I wouldn't be helping you if I thought you did. Although I should turn you in just for scaring me like that. How long were you hiding in those woods?"

"A friend dropped me off there an hour ago."

"What if I hadn't been parked so close to the woods?"

"Then I would have had to hot-wire a car and get

the hell out of town. I'm only trusting you because the message came through Erna."

"Why didn't you leave town?"

"I tried. Got as far as Chicago, but there were cops there watching all the outgoing buses. That's when I decided to call Erna. She said if I didn't kill anyone I should come back here and let you help me. What she said made sense. I don't want to spend the rest of my life running from the cops for a murder I didn't commit. I should have known that Wright dame was going to be trouble."

"How did you get involved with her?"

"Leona slipped me a few bucks to take her to Wright's house. Said she was going to interview him. He wasn't at home, but Madeline was there and agreed to talk to Leona."

"After she talked to Madeline, did Leona seem disturbed by the interview?"

"Not at all."

"Then what made you steal the tape?"

Peter laughed. "That was Madeline Wright's idea. She offered me twenty-five hundred bucks to get the tape and use it to blackmail her husband. Said we could get a bundle from him and split it."

"Why was she at your apartment that night?"

Dana gazed in the rearview mirror at Peter. He was shaking his head as he remembered the events of that fateful night. "She showed up there all upset about some fight she had with her husband. She wanted a drink and since I didn't have anything but beer, she sent me out to buy her a bottle of whiskey, Southern Comfort to be exact. When I got back with the booze, I heard the gunshot. I figured her husband had followed her there, so I got the hell out of there."

"You didn't stay around to see who came out of your apartment?"

"No. I should have called the cops right then and there, but I was scared. And if you'd heard Madeline talk about her husband, you would have run too."

Dana nodded. With the new information she had on Templeton and Hatterly, there was a chance that the two murders were not connected, or there was the possibility that Charles Wright, the handsome, charming candidate was a cold-blooded killer who had killed two women. Then again, Hogan could be lying to save his own skin. "So, you think Charles Wright killed his wife?"

"I did until I heard that the cops found the tape and stuff that proved I was blackmailing him. Why would he leave it behind?"

"Maybe he didn't think it would be as damaging to his image as being arrested for murder," Dana replied. "I'd like to hear that tape. Do you have another copy of it?"

"What makes you think I have another copy?"

"Making a duplicate tape would be the smart thing to do."

"If I were smart, I wouldn't be in this mess," Peter said. "Hey, I'm starving. I hope you got some food at your apartment."

Dana opened her purse and took out the chocolate chip cookies she had saved from dinner at Peaceful Pines. She passed them back to Peter. “Here. Now what about that duplicate tape? If I’m going to help you, I have to know everything.”

Peter took the cookies and shoved one into his mouth. When he was done chewing he spoke again. “Madeline took care of the tape. I only delivered it to her and made the phone calls to Wright. If there’s a duplicate, it’s in the package she had me put in a locker at the bus station.”

TWENTY-SIX

DANA PARKED HER CAR on the street in front of her building. "I'll go in the front and turn on the lights. You go around and come up the back stairs."

A few minutes later, Hogan was settled at Dana's counter eating a sandwich while she set up her own tape recorder. Peter's jacket was hung over the back of the fancy high-backed oak stool that matched the kitchen cabinets.

Dana had Peter repeat everything he had told her in the car. With the tape still running she had him tell her about the locker where he had hidden the original tape.

"It's at the Greyhound station, locker 5235."

"Key please," Dana said, holding out her hand as she turned off the tape recorder.

Hogan shrugged and reached for his jacket. He dug around in his pockets and came up with a set of keys. He removed a small key from the ring and handed it to Dana. The number 5235 was stamped on one side of the silver key.

Dana dropped the key into the pocket of her slacks and began to clean up the plate and napkins from Hogan's late-night snack.

"I could use a drink. You got any beer?"

Dana nodded and went to the refrigerator. There was an unopened six-pack that Bruno had brought over a few days earlier. She snapped off a can from the plastic carrier and handed it to Hogan.

Bruno would have a fit if he knew Hogan was in her apartment. If he knew Hogan was drinking his beer he would probably shoot him on the spot.

Unaware of the danger, Peter pushed aside the water Dana had provided with his sandwich and opened the beer. He took a long drink, then put the can down and took a deck of cards from his jacket pocket and shook the playing cards out of the box and began shuffling them.

Dana watched as he deftly dealt out the framework for a game of solitaire. "Where did those cards come from?" she asked suspiciously.

"I found these in Leona's case. They're probably the ones I was using to teach her and Helen how to play poker. They were catching on pretty good, until Erna came along and lectured me about neglecting my other duties. Entertaining those sweet old gals was the one thing I liked about that job. The rest of it sucked."

"From what I've gathered, the old gals were pretty fond of you," Dana told him. "That's one of the things that convinced me that you weren't a murderer."

"Erna says Helen is still in the hospital. Damn shame. I hope she comes out of it all right."

"I think she's getting better," Dana said. "Okay,

you stay put here. I'm going to the bus station to get that tape. Don't answer the phone or the door. I'll be back as soon as I can."

Hogan nodded and began to play the hand of solitaire he had dealt himself, turning over the cards slowly. Dana scooped up the tape recorder she had just used to record Hogan's statement and headed for the door.

She would drop Hogan's tape off at the newspaper office for safekeeping. She would type up a statement from it, and include the information she had gathered from the residents at Peaceful Pines. If the tape at the bus station proved to be useful, she would turn everything over to the police. Hopefully, it would be enough to get Hogan off the hook and turn the focus to other suspects who had motives to kill Leona and Madeline Wright.

The bus station was on the other side of town, so Dana stopped at the newspaper office first. She locked her recorder and tape into her desk drawer and hurried off again.

It was almost midnight by the time Dana returned to her apartment. After listening to Leona's original tape in her car outside the bus station, she had taken it directly to *The Globe* and locked it into her desk with the tape of Hogan's interview.

The voices of Leona and Madeline Wright were still echoing in her head when she parked her car and walked toward her building. The information on the original tape had made a trip to Florida unnecessary.

The possibility of spending a few hours on a beach enjoying a warm ocean breeze was disappearing, but the satisfaction of knowing she was right about this case made up for it.

Now she needed to focus on Peter Hogan and what she would say to him. She had to convince him to go to the police station with her and turn himself in.

She entered the building and ran up the few stairs that led from the lobby to the landing for the first floor. She turned the corner to climb the flight of stairs leading to her apartment and stopped dead in her tracks.

Bruno was sitting on the stairs. Dana gasped.

"Damn it, Bruno. You scared the hell out of me. What are you doing here?"

"My car is in the lot. Didn't you see it?"

"No." Dana had been too busy thinking about Leona's tape and what she was going to say to Hogan to notice anything else around here.

"And I suppose you forgot that you invited me to dinner?"

"Don't be crazy," Dana told him. "It's almost midnight."

"Good thing I already ate," he said calmly. "Then I saw the latest edition of your newspaper and got acidita."

Dana didn't reply. She was thinking of Peter Hogan hiding out in her apartment and how close Bruno was to finding out he was there. She wanted Peter to go to the police, but she didn't want the police to know she had been harboring a murder suspect. She especially didn't want Bruno to know Hogan was there drinking his beer.

"When are you and your crew going to stop meddling in police business?" Bruno said in the same calm voice.

"We work for a newspaper, Bruno. It's our job to meddle." *That's why I have Hogan in my apartment as we speak,* she thought. *I'm just doing my job.*

"I should haul you down to the station right now and charge you with obstructing a police investigation," Bruno told her.

"That's ridiculous," Dana retorted. "You're just mad because Casey came up with a better idea than you and all the other cops on this case."

"I'm mad because you didn't consult me before printing this story."

"I tried to tell you at lunch. It's not my fault you had to answer a call. Besides, the only person I have to consult on a story is my editor."

"You're not a cop, Dana, so stop trying to act like one."

"Okay, you're right," Dana said. "From now on I'll clear all my stories with you first."

Bruno smiled. "Yeah, right, and the Pope is going to call me and ask my opinion on celibacy."

"You keep harassing me and you're going to become an expert on the subject, at least as far as I'm concerned. Now I'm tired. Good night."

Dana tried to walk around him, but he blocked

her way. "Hang on, honey. I'm off duty. Now that we've had an argument I think we should go upstairs together and make up."

"I can't do that."

"Why not?"

"I have something I have to do at *The Globe*. I'm going back there."

Dana was improvising, trying to get Bruno out of the building and away from her apartment and Hogan. Her tone must have been a little too desperate because even when she turned to descend the stairs to the lobby, he didn't budge.

"What's in your apartment that you don't want me to see?"

Dana forced a smile. "Don't be silly. I was going to stop in my apartment and change, but now you've made me late, so I have to go."

Dana ran down the steps, but before she could get the door open, Bruno was next to her, taking hold of her.

"I don't believe you. Who's up there?"

"No one," Dana insisted. "Now get out of my way. I have a story to file."

"I don't think so." With one deft movement, Bruno picked Dana up and threw her over his shoulder.

"Are you nuts? Put me down, Bruno."

Bruno ignored her and began to trudge up the stairs, holding her firmly in place against his shoulder.

"I'm going to start screaming," Dana warned.

"Go ahead," Bruno replied. "Maybe someone will call a cop." Reaching her door, Bruno set her down. "Open it."

"Go to hell," Dana whispered.

"See," Bruno said cheerfully. "That proves you've got someone in there. Otherwise, you would unlock the damn door just to prove me wrong."

"I'm not opening the damn door because I don't want to open the damn door. And you're not going to make me, you big fat bully." Dana glared at him.

Bruno stared at the door as if he were thinking about breaking it down. Dana stood her ground. Then, Bruno touched the door with his finger and it swung open.

"Looks like your boyfriend made a quick get-away," Bruno said.

Dana pushed past him into the apartment. The lights were still on. In the kitchen, Hogan's jacket was still hanging off the back of the stool, but he was nowhere in sight. Dana ran out of the kitchen to search the bedroom and bathroom. No luck. Hogan was gone.

She returned to the kitchen to find Bruno holding Hogan's jacket.

"It's my brother's," Dana said quickly.

Bruno held up an identification badge from Peaceful Pines. It had Peter Hogan printed in bold black letters across the front of it.

"You have the right to remain silent. You have the right—"

"Shut up, Bruno," Dana yelled. "This is no time for jokes. We have to find him."

Bruno continued to recite the Miranda warning, until screams from the street below stopped him. Drawing his gun, he bounded through the apartment and down the front stairs. Dana was right behind him.

Two teenage girls were standing beside the building, staring over the shrubbery that lined the parking lot and the walkway that led to the back of the building. Dana recognized one of them as the daughter of the first-floor tenants. Their screams had dissolved into sobs and now the other tenants were beginning to emerge from the building.

Dana followed Bruno around the shrubbery to the walkway. There, lying in the grassy area alongside the walkway, was Peter Hogan.

The security lights from the building illuminated the grisly scene. Peter was facedown, his right hand still loosely clutching the gun that had most likely made the large hole in the right side of his head. On the left side of the body was a deck of cards. They were bunched together as if he had been holding them in his hand and dropped them when he fell.

TWENTY-SEVEN

SERGEANT MILECKI AND DANA were alone in the interrogation room. Milecki had lost his flirty, friendly attitude.

Bruno had ordered one of the officers to take Dana down to the station and book her for aiding and abetting a fugitive. Milecki had been called in to question her, since he was supposed to be an impartial party from another district.

"One more time, Miss Sloan," Milecki said. "What was Peter Hogan doing in your apartment?"

"He was having a sandwich."

"How do you explain that?"

"I guess he was hungry."

Milecki tried to suppress his smile, but didn't quite succeed. "You're not going to talk, are you?" he asked.

"Not until Sam gets here with my lawyer," Dana replied. "And you shouldn't even be in here asking me questions. It will taint the case against me."

Milecki grinned. "Hey, come on, Dana. You know Bruno is just pissed, trying to teach you a lesson."

Dana heard footsteps in the hall, and a moment later, Bruno barged through the door. "The cards on Hogan match up with the ones found on victim number five. They'll have a report on the gun within an hour."

"I'm betting it matched up too," Milecki said.

Dana jumped to her feet. "Don't tell me you honestly believe Peter Hogan is the Royal Flush killer. His description doesn't even match what the witnesses saw at the last killing."

Bruno turned and faced her. His dark eyes were cold and menacing. "Sit down. No one was talking to you."

Dana remained standing. "Why would he come to me for help then go outside and commit suicide? It doesn't make sense."

"You're the one who doesn't make sense," Bruno said in an icy tone. "It's time you learned that freedom of the press doesn't mean you can break the law and get away with it."

Dana's back stiffened as she returned his glare. "You're letting your anger at me cloud your judgment. I told you Hogan said the cards he had came from Leona's case. Don't you understand what that means?"

Milecki got up to join the argument. "It means that Hogan lied to you, little lady. And when he saw Bruno's car outside your apartment, he realized that he had no other place to run, so he took the easy way out. You're lucky he didn't blow his brains out inside your apartment."

Dana took a deep breath, and turned to the other detective. "That is the dumbest..."

Milecki was spared from hearing the rest of the insult by the arrival of Sam McGowan, who burst into the room unannounced.

"What's this nonsense about holding my reporter?" Sam directed the question to Bruno.

"I'm going to check with the lab," Milecki said as he made a fast exit. Apparently he had decided that the room had become too crowded.

Bruno looked at Sam and suddenly decided to follow Milecki's lead. "I'll give you five minutes to talk to your reporter before I lock her in a cell."

The door slammed behind the detectives. Sam turned his attention to Dana. "I've called our attorney. What else can I do?"

"Help me get out of here."

"Are you crazy?" Sam whispered. "Bruno is mad as hell. He's going to throw the book at you."

"I can't worry about that now," Dana whispered back. "I've got to get to the hospital and talk to Helen Johnson."

"They're not going to let us in there at this time of night."

"They have to," Dana said. Her tone was desperate. "Listen to me, Sam. Peter Hogan had a deck of cards the Royal Flush killer used on victim number five. Bruno just confirmed it. Hogan told me the cards came from Peaceful Pines. He found them in Leona's tape recorder case. We have to get to the hospital and find out if Helen knows anything about this."

"You've got to explain this to Bruno," Sam told her.

"I tried to, but he's not listening to anything I say. Now are you going to help me or not?"

Sam nodded and went to the door. Opening it slowly, he peered down the corridor outside the interrogation room. It was empty. Silently, he motioned for Dana to follow him and they slipped out of the room.

Sam and Dana had both worked the police beat and knew their way around the station. Hurrying down the hallway, Sam pushed through a door at the end of the corridor and led Dana down a stairway.

The evidence department was located in the basement of the station. Sam was betting that the officer on duty down there was not aware of Dana's arrest. Luck was with them. The cop on duty was the same guy who had provided Dana with information a few days earlier when Wright had been taken into custody.

"Hey, McGowan," the cop said when Sam and Dana passed by him. "When are you going to cough up those tickets you owe me?"

"They're in the works," Sam promised. "You'll have them before the next home game."

"Great. Good seats, right?"

"Great seats," Sam replied. "Can you buzz us through to the street? It's a madhouse upstairs."

"Sure," the cop said with a friendly wave. "See you later."

He pushed a button and the lock on the steel door that led to a set of stairs behind the station clicked. Sam and Dana hurried through it.

It was almost 2:00 a.m. and the air was so cold it made Dana shiver. Sam grabbed her arm and scooted around a corner and then they ran for his car.

Sam cranked the engine and they sped away from the police station and headed for the hospital.

They entered the hospital through the emergency entrance and took the elevator up to Helen's floor. The nurses on duty were laughing and talking among themselves at the station and didn't even glance at Sam and Dana as they approached Helen's room and slipped inside.

Helen's room was lit only by the moonlight shining in from outside. The covers on the bed were drawn up partially covering Helen's face. Sam moved to the bed while Dana switched on a small light on the bedside table.

"Helen," Sam said softly, not wanting to startle the old woman.

When she didn't respond, Sam moved the blanket from her face and called out to her again.

"They probably gave her a sedative," Dana said. She pulled the blanket down a little more intending to shake the old woman's arm.

The sheet underneath the blanket was soaked with blood. Helen Johnson would not be able to answer any of Dana's questions. Helen Johnson was dead, murdered while she slept.

Sam cursed softly under his breath. Dana backed away from the bed, and stood frozen in place while she tried to make sense of all that she had learned in the last few weeks.

Sam turned to look at his reporter. "Come on, let's get out of here."

TWENTY-EIGHT

CHARLES AND PAULETTE were sequestered inside the limousine with the tinted windows. It was late. They had enjoyed a midnight dinner at one of Chicago's upscale all-night restaurants. They were on their way back to Pine Grove City, opting to go home rather than spend another night in a hotel.

They had been working all day, making unannounced stops at shopping malls, setting up tables where they handed out campaign literature and Charles talked to as many people as possible. His feet were aching, his hand was numb from shaking hands, and his mind had gone on autopilot a few hours earlier.

Even as he worked to influence voters, Charles wondered if any politician honestly thought all this effort was worth it. He certainly didn't. He already had wealth. He didn't need a job, and being the governor of a state as populated as Illinois would indeed be a job, a huge job. He was knocking himself out for a job he didn't even want.

Running for political office had not been his idea. It had been forced upon him by a very select group of business associates. Madeline had known and fought against it. Her resistance had led her to a flower-filled grave.

For the last hour or so, Wright had been thinking a lot about Madeline. Perhaps because so many people he met now expressed their sympathy to him.

"A beautiful woman." "You have great courage to carry on without her." "God bless you in your time of grief." On and on the remarks went, until Charles wanted to throw his hands in the air and yell at them to shut up.

Now in the back of the limousine, with Paulette cuddled against him, sound asleep, Wright had given up the fight and allowed himself to think about Madeline and the days when they had been happy. It was a long time ago, and it was painful to think about those days, but the more he let the thoughts in, the more they kept coming.

"How long before you'll try to get me into your bed?" Madeline had asked the first time they danced together.

"That's up to you," he had answered quietly.

Her hair was brown then, its natural color. She was a drama major at the university where Charles was following his father's wishes and studying law.

He was attracted by her beauty and entranced by her open, free-spirited personality. Unlike Charles, Madeline never tried to impress people, never worried about what others thought of her. She just did or said whatever popped into her mind, and of course that coupled with her exquisite looks never failed to win people over.

They had known each other for a month. Madeline had the female lead in a silly drama production written by another student who was obviously smitten with his star. Charles had a very minor role. He was taking drama as an elective, not really interested in performing, but thinking that being on stage in front of an audience would be good experience for someone who hoped to be a trial lawyer.

Opening night had been a dismal failure, and the cast and crew had gone to a bar to drown their sorrows. The bar had a jukebox and when a slow song began to play, Madeline had asked Charles to dance.

"You're not a fake," Madeline said, squeezing the muscle in his arm. "Some football players are nothing without the padding in their uniforms, but you've got the real stuff."

"Maybe you'd like to see more," Charles replied, pulling her closer.

"Maybe I would."

They had stayed together that night, and every night for two weeks afterward. By the end of the semester, they were engaged. They got married the week after graduation.

Charles went to law school at Pepperdine and Madeline came along with him. Malibu, California, was the perfect place for her to make the contacts she needed to launch a film career.

They were happy back then. Charles was never a nose-to-the-grindstone type of student. He had learned to use his good looks and charm to get ahead, and that soon led to opportunities that were lucrative, and a bit underhanded.

Madeline worked hard trying to establish her career. Charles often thought if she had been single then, she would have become a movie star. Having a husband was a hindrance as Madeline tried to juggle her responsibilities as his wife with the time and energy she needed to pursue an acting career.

After he got his law degree, they returned to Pine Grove City. Madeline was disillusioned with Hollywood. She had decided to give up acting to become a mother.

Unfortunately, Madeline was not able to become pregnant. While his wife fretted about the child she could not have, and spent thousands of dollars on specialists, Charles concentrated on earning money. He was an associate at a prestigious Chicago law firm.

It was there that he became friendly with the people who were responsible for his wife's death, business associates who worked their way into every aspect of his life. They had shown him quick, easy ways to accumulate money and he had gone along, enjoying the challenge and even the risks. Madeline had warned him, had pleaded with him to walk away from the deals they offered, the businesses they wanted him to run. At the same time, she had enjoyed the money and the luxuries it afforded them.

When it was evident that she would never be able to give birth to her own child, Madeline was devastated. She went into a depression that lasted for several months. When Charles confided this to his associates, they had a solution. They promised to help Madeline find success in another endeavor. They would help her establish her acting career.

"It will be good therapy for you," Charles had said at the time. Little did he know that this would be the thing that ultimately destroyed her.

His associates sent Madeline to the best photographers for headshots, professional photos used by actors and models. Arrangements were made with a top talent agent. Madeline was happy again. She expected instant fame, and she might have gotten it, if there had not been a threat to the structure of the organization built by their benefactors.

The downward spiral began when a congressman who had been doing favors for them died unexpectedly. Papers found at his house caused a shake-up that spread across the state. Politicians were resigning and leaving the state faster than the paper shredder could eliminate evidence.

Some of it was still going on. Just a few weeks ago, that *Globe* reporter who worked with Dana Sloan had unearthed some additional facts that sent some Crescent Hills politicians running for cover.

"They want me to run for governor," Charles had announced at dinner one night.

"You don't have any political experience," Madeline had said casually, not yet realizing what would be required of her.

"It doesn't matter. I have a law degree, so it is assumed that I know the law and can successfully manage the state's business."

"Okay. If that's what you want," Madeline said.

"I don't have a choice, Madeline. I have to do this."

"They're forcing you?"

"Let's just say, they want me to do it so badly I'm afraid to refuse."

"What if you lose the election?"

"I don't know. They're confident that my looks and reputation will make me a sure thing. They control the party, so my nomination will be easy enough."

Madeline had suddenly caught on. "Most candidates have a doting spouse at their side. I can't do that. I'm up for that part at Universal. I'll be on location for months."

Charles could not bring himself to tell her. She wasn't going to get the part. It had already been taken from her. It didn't take her more than a few seconds to catch on.

"It's not fair. They promised me, now they're taking it all back."

"They have high expectations for both of us. As

the governor's wife, you'll have as much, maybe more prestige..."

Madeline didn't let him finish. "I won't do it, Charles. And you shouldn't either. They are using you. You'll be under public scrutiny. It's a huge risk. Reporters will be looking at us like bugs under a microscope. If your association with them comes out, you could even go to jail."

Charles was well aware of those possibilities, but he was not in a position to deny his friends' wishes.

Madeline stubbornly refused to go along. At first, she vowed to establish her acting career without them. The next morning she called her agent, but he refused to talk to her. A few days later, she received a letter saying the agency had dropped her.

Over the next few weeks, Madeline went to California and New York trying to make connections on her own. She failed.

Charles feared that she would go into another depression, but instead, she went into a simmering rage. She refused to be seen in public with him, refused to do anything to help him in his bid for political office.

Charles tried to reason with her, but she wouldn't listen. As the days and weeks passed, she became more and more bitter and uncooperative. She took long vacations without him.

His friends were very concerned, and Charles assured them over and over that Madeline's lack of cooperation was due to poor health, that she was not a threat to them or the campaign.

They brought in Paulette to take Madeline's place. Charles knew that she was controlled by them, just as he was.

Still, Charles tried to protect Madeline. He had pleaded with her to do what they wanted, but she would not listen.

"They're not going to touch me," Madeline told him. "I've got the goods on them and you. If something happens to me, it's over for all of you. You go tell them that."

Charles had not told them. He was too afraid of what they might do, but in the end, Madeline had gone crazy. She had talked to that old reporter. She had even tried to blackmail him. At that point, Charles had no choice. He had to tell Paulette.

Paulette was with him all the time. She watched him like a hawk. She said she was in love with him, but Charles knew that their affair was simply a way to be with him all night as well as all day. He couldn't slip out and pay blackmail money without her finding out. He was trapped. If he tried to make a move behind the backs of his friends, he had no doubt that they would kill him.

Charles had taken Madeline out to the garden that last night, just a few hours before she died. He tried again to make her see how much danger she was putting them in. She laughed and denied knowing anything about the man and the blackmail demand.

"I'm going back to Florida. Sorry I won't be here to vote for you."

He had slapped her. She had screamed obscenities at him and fled.

Paulette stirred beside him. She was an attractive woman, very adept at pleasing a man. Charles was relatively sure that if he got elected, they would instruct him to marry Paulette—if he lived long enough to get elected.

His only hope was that Madeline had been bluffing when she said information would surface if something happened to her. That was the one thing Charles had not told anyone. To admit it now would surely get him killed. His friends all had safe havens in foreign lands where they could hide indefinitely. Charles had only two places he could go, jail or the cemetery.

It had been several days now and nothing had happened. Peter Hogan had disappeared. Charles could only hope that he never reappeared.

For a while he had thought Madeline's murder would cause him to lose the election, but the voters seemed to like him more now. Paulette had been right. Madeline's murder had gained more supporters for him. He would never escape from them. They controlled his life.

The telephone rang. Paulette jerked to attention and reached for it.

"Hello." She listened for several minutes, without saying anything. Then she smiled. "How perfect. Thank you."

"What is it?" Charles asked.

"Peter Hogan committed suicide right in Dana Sloan's backyard."

"He killed himself?"

"It looks that way. But that's not the best part. The police think he's the Royal Flush killer. Isn't that too perfect?"

Relief flooded over Charles. Perhaps it would be all right. Perhaps all of Madeline's threats had died with her and Hogan.

TWENTY-NINE

IN THE LOBBY, Dana and Sam emerged from the elevator and began making their way back to the emergency room area and the exit. After they passed by a public phone hanging on the wall, Sam stopped walking. Everything was quiet.

"We'd better call the police and report Helen's murder," Sam said, taking his cell phone out of his overcoat pocket. "We should have alerted the nurses."

"The nurses?" A look of confusion came over Dana's face, then it changed to understanding. "Oh my God." Dana staggered and grabbed hold of Sam's arm for support. "Sam, I know who the Royal Flush killer is. Helen was trying to tell us all along. We just didn't get it."

"What?" Sam voice echoed loudly in the eerily quiet corridor. They were standing in a hallway lined with offices that had been closed for hours.

"Leona's death didn't have anything to do with Madeline Wright. She and Helen and Peter Hogan stumbled into the path of the Royal Flush killer. The Royal Flush killer is a woman, one of the nurses at Peaceful Pines."

"Are you sure?"

"No, but it makes sense and we have to check it out. Hurry and call Bruno. I have to call Templeton." Dana opened her bag and started rummaging around for her cell phone. "Damn it, I think I left my phone in my car."

"Here, use mine." Sam held out his phone. "I'll use the public phone back there."

Dana took the phone and continued to search her bag for the card she had on Templeton. Finding his home phone number she quickly dialed it. Sam disappeared around the corner to use the public telephone they had just passed.

Tapping her foot impatiently, Dana waited for the call to connect. When it did, she spoke urgently, but calmly. "Mr. Templeton, this is Dana Sloan. I'm sorry to wake you, but it's an emergency. Two of your residents may be in danger, Dr. Mary Powers and Rocky Colosimo. I think they have information on the Royal Flush killer. I need you to alert your security staff." Dana paused as she listened to Templeton sputtering on the other end. "I don't have time to argue. Just do as I say. And then get to Peaceful Pines. I'll meet you there with the police."

Dana broke off the connection and dropped the phone and the card into her purse. Before she could turn around and join Sam at the public phone, a strong hand grabbed her arm and twisted it behind her back.

Dana gasped with surprise and pain as the sharp

point of a knife was pressed against the side of her neck. "Do not scream or I will kill you here," a voice whispered.

"Sam is calling the police," Dana replied quietly.

"He spoke to no one," the knife wielder with a hint of a German accent told her. Dana was propelled forward and pushed around the corner.

Sam was lying in a heap against the wall. Blood was oozing from his body. The phone was dangling by its cord. Dana let out a small soft cry.

"He called them before, from Helen's room," Dana lied. "They will be here any second."

"But we will be gone," Erna said casually. Pushing Dana forward, she steered her down the corridor and out the emergency room door to the back of the hospital.

Dana looked around frantically for help. She could hear the voices of the hospital's emergency room staff as they tended to patients, but no one was in view of the doorway.

"Where's an ambulance when you need it?" Dana said, sarcastically.

"Shut up," Erna replied.

Outside, Erna walked Dana around the side of the hospital to an alleyway. It was a narrow dark space filled with garbage cans. Steel security doors that led to the back corridors of the hospital were closed and locked.

Erna backed Dana against a wall between an assortment of metal garbage cans and Dumpsters and let go of her. The stocky dark-clad nurse kept the knife against Dana's throat. A trickle of blood was making its way down to the collar of Dana's jacket.

"Why didn't you just kill me in there?" Dana asked.

"This is a more private place. No one likes to come into alleys, only the bums like my husband."

"Is that why you killed all those men, because they reminded you of your husband?" Dana asked quietly. She was stalling for time, hoping to think of some way to catch Erna off guard.

Erna didn't need much encouragement. She wanted to tell her story. "They were all like maggots, living off of garbage and leaving their families to do the same. Drinking and gambling is all that matters to them. My husband took the last of our money to use for his card games. He left me home with our boy, a sick little boy, who died crying for his papa."

"I'm sorry," Dana told her. "I didn't know that you lost a child."

"There is much you do not know. Later, I found his father, drinking and playing cards with his friends. When I told him our boy was dead, he laughed and said I was lying to get him to come home. One night, I waited for him in the alley by our house. When I stuck the knife in him and saw his blood spurt out, it washed away some of my pain and so it has been with the others. Their blood pays for the life of my boy."

"Yes, of course," Dana said. "I can see how you were driven to do this."

"You see nothing. You meddle and ask questions, but you see nothing. I have a mission. I am eliminating worthless men who are a disgrace and embarrassment to decent people." Tears misted Erna's frantic eyes. "I did not want to hurt Leona and Helen, but that stupid Peter took the cards from my desk to teach them poker. When I tried to get them back, Leona would not give them up. Later, I heard her on the phone with her editor talking about the big story."

"So you killed her."

Erna nodded. "Yes, but Peter had gotten to her room before me that night. He took her case where she had put the cards."

"Erna, he was only interested in the tape of Madeline Wright. She paid him to steal it. He found the cards, but he didn't know what they meant."

"No, but tonight when I saw the newspaper article, I knew that if you talked to Peter you might figure it all out."

Dana couldn't move for fear of the knife cutting deeper into her throat. She tried to reason with Erna. "Listen to me. You are not responsible for the things you have done. I can help you."

Erna laughed at her. "You are a liar. You do not wish to help me. You wish only to get the big story, like Leona, like your editor."

"Like Helen?" Dana asked. Erna just stared back at her. The tears were gone now—only the rage remained. "That's why she kept ringing for the nurse every time Sam or I questioned her. She was trying to tell us that a nurse murdered Leona. I was foolish enough to tell you that earlier tonight." Dana closed her eyes, horrified that her trust in Erna had led to Helen's death.

"Don't take credit, Dana. Helen should have been dead before Leona," she said coldly.

"You caused her to have that stroke."

"Yes, the day that they took the cards, I began substituting her blood pressure medicine with sugar pills. But she still brought you to cause me more trouble. That's why I had to wait to kill Peter. You were too close. He was a fool. He called me from your apartment and told me how you promised to help him. You are the last loose end. When I kill you, all my trouble will be over. I will move on to another town and a new beginning."

Dana strained her ears trying to discern the sound of a car or something, anything to distract Erna. There was only silence and the sound of her own blood pounding inside her head. She had to keep Erna talking. "How many towns have you been in, Erna? How many men have you killed?"

Erna smiled and shrugged her shoulders. "Many towns, many men, but no one else until here. It was the cards. I should not have left the cards."

Erna moved back a fraction of an inch as she contemplated her mistake with the playing cards. Dana brought her hands up and pushed against the middle of Erna's stomach, causing her to stumble backward a bit farther.

Grabbing a lid from a garbage can, Dana used it as a shield to stop the knife that Erna struck out with. As she tried to duck away, Erna lunged at her and the knife slashed across Dana's arm cutting through her jacket and slicing into her upper arm.

Dana screamed, pushed the metal lid into Erna's face and ran. Erna recovered quickly and came after her. Dana grabbed the lid from another garbage can and flung it at Erna, hitting her square in the chest. Then, taking whatever she could put her hands on in the can, started throwing bottles, tin cans and plastic containers.

Erna continued to advance on her. Too late, Dana realized that the alley was a dead end. There was no place for her to run.

Blood was dripping from the wound in her arm, and it hurt like hell. Dana had no choice but to keep throwing things at Erna trying to keep her at bay.

The squad car roared into the alley, lighting up the scene with its headlights. Even that didn't stop Erna—she ran at Dana again. Dana saw the knife flash and tried to move out of the way. She crashed into another line of garbage cans as Bruno grabbed Erna from behind and flung her to the ground.

Suddenly, the alley was filled with people. Erna struggled against the men who were forcing her hands behind her back. She was screaming and shouting obscenities.

Dana was stunned from her collision with the metal garbage cans and felt light-headed from the blood she was losing. Bruno lifted her off her feet and carried her out of the alley and into the hospital.

Without a word he handed her over to an emergency room doctor who was on his way outside to investigate the noise and commotion.

The doctor yelled for assistance and he and a nurse took Dana into a treatment room. Bruno was gone.

"Take it easy, Miss," the nurse instructed. They settled Dana on a table and began cutting off the clothes on her right side, so they could get to the source of the bleeding.

The doctor shouted orders that Dana couldn't understand. She knew that she was going to pass out.

"Sam. You've got to help Sam," Dana said just before everything went black.

THIRTY

WHEN DANA WOKE UP, she was in a room much like the one Helen Johnson had occupied. The morning sun spilled across the bed. Her arm was bandaged from her shoulder to her wrist and she felt like she was floating.

Marianne was sitting in a chair at her bedside. Her flaming red hair made her pale face look ghostly. Dana used her left hand to wave at her.

"You're awake. How do you feel?" Marianne asked, jumping up and moving to Dana's side.

"Sam?" Dana asked in a terrified whisper.

"He's down the hall, running the paper from his hospital bed. He's yelling at everyone. Bob and Casey are running interference between him and the nurses. I decided it was safer to stay with you."

Relief washed over Dana and tears sprang to her eyes. Marianne handed her some tissues from the box on the bedside table.

"Then he's okay?"

"He's in better shape than you are," Marianne assured her. "Only needed a few stitches in his shoulder. He does have a concussion from banging his head on the floor though."

"Thank God," Dana whispered.

"Bruno was here, but you were still sleeping. He told me to call him as soon as you woke up. He was a wreck worrying about you."

"Call the city desk instead. I've got a story to file about the Royal Flush killer."

"Sam already filed the story. He said you can write a feature later to explain the details."

Dana sighed. That was a relief. She wasn't sure she could remember her conversation with Erna. "What about Dr. Mary and Rocky? Are they okay?"

"Your friends at the retirement home are fine. Sam made us check on them first thing. What about Bruno? He made me promise to call him."

"You can call him. Tell him I'm awake and I said thank you for saving my life. Then tell him I said he's a bully and a jerk and I never want to see him again."

"Oh, Dana. You don't mean that."

"I mean every word," Dana said. Then she closed her eyes and went back to sleep.

That night, Dana was allowed out of bed. Bob, who had taken Marianne's place at Dana's bedside, put her in a wheelchair and brought her down to Sam's room. He was sitting up in bed being pampered by his wife. He broke into a huge smile when he saw Dana.

Emily gave Dana a hug, then decided to take Dana's visit as an opportunity to go get some supper. "We sent Marianne home a few minutes ago," she said.

Dana told Bob to go along with her.

"You don't have to tell me twice to get something to eat," Bob said. "But I'm on a diet, so don't let me have dessert."

Emily McGowan rolled her eyes and groaned as they left the room.

"How are you feeling?" Dana asked when she and Sam were alone.

"I'm mad as hell. How about you?"

"Actually, I'm feeling pretty humble. I almost got you killed."

"You're the one who almost got killed. That lunatic woman hit me from behind and then tried to stab me as I went down. Got me in the shoulder instead of a vital organ."

"That's good," Dana told him.

"Have you straightened things out with Bruno?"

"I'm not talking to him. How did he get here anyway?"

"Instead of placing a call and going through the switchboard, I dialed nine-one-one. The woman knocked me out before I could talk, but the nine-one-one system is equipped to know where each incoming call originates. The dispatcher sent the message to the cops. When Bruno discovered we'd skipped, he figured we might be here trying to talk to Helen again and came along with the cops sent to investigate the nine-one-one call."

Dana nodded. "I've got some other information that needs to be passed on to the police," she said.

"About the Royal Flush murders?"

"No. It's about the murder of Madeline Wright."

Sam straightened up, bringing himself to full attention. "You learned something useful from Hogan?"

"Yes, and from the original tape of Leona's interview with Madeline Wright. The tape the police have was altered."

"Well," Sam said with a broad smile. "Sounds like our paper is going to have a story no one else has access to. Tell me about it."

"I'd rather you listen to the tapes. They're both locked in my desk at the paper. How soon can we get out of this place?"

Sam reached for the telephone. "Not soon enough," he said to Dana as he punched in some numbers.

Dana and Sam were scheduled to be released from the hospital the next morning, but Sam called his doctor and convinced the man to come to the hospital that night and sign them out.

Sam's wife wasn't happy about taking him to *The Globe* office instead of home, but after all the years she had spent with Sam she knew that talking him out of it was useless. She compromised by insisting that she go along so she could keep an eye on him.

It was after 8:00 p.m. when Sam, Dana, and Bob locked themselves into Dana's office to play the tapes. Emily had settled into the reception area with one of Marianne's fashion magazines.

First they listened to Dana's interview with Peter Hogan. Dana felt more than a little guilty as she listened to his voice on the tape. If she hadn't asked

Erna to tell Peter to contact her for help, he might have been far away from Crescent Hills and still alive.

When she voiced her feelings, Sam assumed some of the guilt on himself. "If I hadn't asked you to investigate Leona's death, it might not have happened."

"I think you should both remember that Hogan wouldn't have been in danger at all if he hadn't tried to blackmail Wright and then run from a murder scene," Bob said. "Not to mention that he was the one who took the cards from the nurse's desk and put all of the events of the past few weeks into play."

Sam and Dana looked at each other and nodded in agreement. Bob went to the recorder and removed Hogan's tape and inserted Leona's.

The first few minutes of the tape were as Bruno had described them to Dana. A wife, who felt neglected and betrayed by her husband's political ambitions, venting her anger and unhappiness.

Then Leona's voice came across in a firm tone. "I understand that you're unhappy in your marriage, my dear, and no one can blame you. A lovely girl like you deserves much better, but none of what you've told me is sufficient reason to keep your husband out of the Governor's Mansion. Is there something else you'd like to tell me?"

Dana glanced at Sam. His eyes looked misty, but he quickly blinked away his emotions when Madeline Wright answered Leona's question.

"You bet I do. Put Charles Wright in the Governor's Mansion and the infamous Chioto family will actually be running the state of Illinois. Charles spends more time in bed with the Mob than he does with me or Paulette."

"Do you have proof of this?" Leona asked.

"How about documents that show a money laundering process that Charles has been running through some of his so-called legitimate business enterprises and proof that the Chiotos are silent partners in a few other ventures?"

"And you can produce this evidence?" Leona asked.

"Anytime you want," Madeline replied.

"I'll need you to do that," Leona said. "But not just yet. First I have to contact my editor at *The Globe* and see how to proceed."

"It's in a safe deposit box under my maiden name at…"

The tape ended suddenly. Leona was smart enough to know that the exact whereabouts of this evidence should not be revealed on the tape.

"Leona's big story was about Charles Wright," Dana said. "But that's not what got her killed. It was the deck of playing cards she refused to return to Erna, the cards that belonged to the Royal Flush killer. So, you see, Sam, there's no need for you to feel guilty about Leona's death."

"Do you think the evidence that Madeline claimed to have against Wright still exists?" Bob asked.

"Yes," Dana answered. "Look in the bottom of the envelope. There's a key in there. I'm betting it's for the safe deposit box Madeline referred to. The name of the bank isn't on it, but the police can probably trace it."

"I'm going to call Bruno and turn all of this over to him. I think we can depend on him to verify the information without jeopardizing our exclusive. We can't break the story until we determine if Madeline Wright was telling Leona the truth about the evidence she had."

"Regardless of whether Madeline actually had documentation, Leona's tape gives Charles Wright a strong motive for killing his wife," Dana said. She moved her bandaged arm and grimaced in pain.

"I'm going to get Dana home," Bob said. "Casey is already stationed at Dana's apartment ready to play nursemaid."

"Good," Dana said. "If Bruno shows up, Casey will send him packing. Sam, call me when you have verification. I've already dictated most of the story. It won't take Marianne long to transcribe it in the morning."

There was a knock on Dana's office door.

"That's probably my wife. She said she'd give me thirty minutes. Let her in and I'll put in a call to Bruno."

Bob walked to the door and opened it, but instead of Mrs. McGowan, he found Bruno standing there.

"I thought I'd find you here. The hospital said you checked out," Bruno said to Dana.

"Right, and now I'm going home. Come on, Bob." Dana got up from her chair and started for the door.

Bruno held his hands in the air in a gesture of surrender. "Let me take you home. We need to talk."

"Forget it, Bruno," Dana said. "You and I are old news, and we have nothing to talk about."

Bob put his pudgy arm around Dana's shoulder and helped her walk from the office. Bruno turned intending to follow them, but Sam stopped him.

"Wait, Bruno. Dana uncovered some evidence in the Madeline Wright case. You're going to have to check it out right away."

Bruno turned around. "She is really mad at me this time."

"Yeah," Sam agreed. "Arresting your girlfriend is a sure way to screw up the relationship. Now sit down. I'll give you something else to think about."

THIRTY-ONE

A WEEK LATER, Charles Wright and Paulette Mason were in jail. The business associates named in Madeline's papers had mysteriously disappeared. Dana's byline had appeared in *The Globe*'s exclusive story announcing the candidate's connection with organized crime and how that connection had probably led to his wife's murder.

The stitches in Dana's arm had been removed. This was the first morning Dana had been able to drive herself to the office. In the meantime, her staff had been taking turns picking her up and driving her home in the evening.

They had also been fielding the phone messages that Bruno was leaving at home and at the office. Every time one was delivered to Dana in writing, she crumpled up the paper and threw it in the trash. So far, Bruno hadn't appeared in person and Dana wasn't sure if she was relieved or disappointed.

"It's time for the news," Marianne announced at noon. She went over and switched on the television.

Dana looked up from the paperwork she was shuffling to watch it.

The camera was focused on a courtroom where

people were exiting into a crowded hallway. The television reporter was a young man Marianne had dated a few times.

"There's Tommy," Dana said. "He looks good."

"He's very handsome," Marianne said. "But Greg is much better company."

Dana smiled. "Bob is already making wedding plans for you two."

"Bob is crazy. We are not that serious." She grinned. "Yet."

Tommy began to make his report. "Just minutes ago, the Grand Jury returned indictments against gubernatorial candidate Charles Wright and his campaign manager Paulette Mason. Miss Mason is charged with first degree murder in the death of Madeline Wright. Charles Wright has been charged an as accessory in the murder. Earlier, the candidate was also indicted on charges of racketeering and money laundering.

"The indictments are based in part on evidence contained in an audio tape. The full contents of the tape have not been disclosed, but it is believed to provide Mason's motive for murdering Madeline Wright."

"And I was going to vote for him," Marianne said as she switched off the television.

"I guess his opponent will win by default."

"Do you think they have enough to convict Wright?" Marianne asked.

"I don't know," Dana replied. "That depends on

the type of evidence Madeline Wright had stashed in that safe deposit box. Sam said they think Paulette went to Hogan's apartment and did the actual killing. Apparently she and Wright didn't know about the safe deposit box."

"Maybe Paulette was just killing Madeline so she would have Wright all to herself."

"Maybe. Paulette was never a suspect, so the police weren't trying to place her at the scene, but once they read the documents and found out that she was also connected to organized crime, they found a witness who saw her in Hogan's neighborhood that night."

"Did Hogan tell you that he erased part of the tape?"

"No. I'm not sure he even listened to it. Madeline was calling the shots. She probably erased the one in the recorder, knowing there was another copy of it in the locker at the bus station."

"I don't understand why Paulette didn't take the tape after she killed Madeline."

"She may have listened to the tape and thought it was a good idea to leave it behind because it would incriminate Hogan. Bruno always says murderers get tripped up by their own mistakes."

"Speaking of Bruno, are you ever going to call him back?"

"No."

"What if he shows up here?"

"He hasn't so far."

"Only because Bob told him that he needed to give

you time to cool down," Marianne admitted. "Now every time he calls, he asks me if I think you're ready to talk to him."

"Enough about Bruno," Dana said firmly. "Here are some problems that need research."

Marianne dutifully took the stack of correspondence Dana held out to her and headed for the door. Once there, she turned around to face her boss again. "Maybe Bob can fix you up with somebody nice."

Dana couldn't help laughing. "I may have to look into that."

That night, Dana came home and changed into her most comfortable pair of sweats. She called her mom and gave her a report on her arm, which was healing nicely. She promised to come home for a visit the coming weekend.

"I'll make all your favorites. Are you going to bring Bruno?" her mother asked.

"I don't think so, Mom," Dana said. "He'll probably have to work."

She hung up and thought about why she was reluctant to tell her mom that she and Bruno were no longer a couple. *It's better to tell her in person,* Dana decided. *She'll have a million questions that I'm not up to answering at the moment.*

After feasting on a microwave dinner, Dana flopped down in front of the television set to watch an old movie.

About halfway through it, her doorbell rang.

Dana went to the door and looked through her

peephole. Bruno was standing in the hall with a bouquet of flowers.

"Dana, I know you're in there," Bruno shouted. "Come on, open the door."

Dana opened the door and Bruno held out the flowers. Dana took them and threw them down the stairs. She then attempted to close the door on Bruno, but he had his foot firmly wedged in the doorway.

"I got your message and came right over," he said.

"I didn't leave you a message."

"But you wanted to," Bruno said hopefully.

"Bruno, the only message I'd leave for you would be to take your oversized male ego for a swim in Lake Michigan."

Dana walked away from the door and Bruno came inside the apartment and closed the door behind him. "The water's kind of cold this time of year, but if that will make you happy I'll do it. Did you want to come along and watch my ego sink to the bottom of the lake?"

Dana glared at him. "Is that supposed to be an apology?"

"I've apologized a hundred times—to your editor, your secretary, your staff, and anyone else you had screening your calls. Now I'm here to talk out our problems, which you started by harboring a fugitive and concealing evidence."

"I solved two murder cases and let you take credit for both of them," Dana yelled.

"You broke the law," Bruno yelled back.

"So I suppose you're sorry you dropped the charges against me. You here to arrest me again?"

"I want to take you into custody, all right," Bruno said in a softer tone. "But only if you promise not to resist."

Bruno held out his arms and Dana grabbed a pillow from the sofa and swung it at him, hitting him in the side of the face.

"You big baboon. Admit that I gave you the case against Charles Wright and Paulette Mason."

"You made the case against them, and you caught the Royal Flush killer too. Or maybe she caught you. I'm not quite clear on that."

Dana tried not to smile. "Get out of here."

"How's your arm?"

"It's a constant reminder of an insane killer, and what can happen when you trust the wrong person," Dana told him.

"Well, being a lady gangbuster isn't easy," Bruno replied. He was about to say more, but Dana attempted to shove him toward the door. Bruno didn't budge, so she gave up and decided to ignore him instead.

She walked out of the room into the kitchen. Opening the refrigerator, she took out a pitcher of orange juice and poured herself a glass. She was sitting at the counter sipping the juice when Bruno joined her.

He took a place on the opposite side of the counter

so they were face-to-face. "As I was about to say," he told her, "you do the best you can, but sometimes people get hurt. It's not your fault, it just happens."

"Thank you. For a minute I thought you were going to give me that speech about cooking pasta and nursing babies."

"That's not a speech, it's a proposal of marriage, and the offer still stands."

Dana sighed and took another sip of juice. "Look, Bruno, tonight you want to make up, but tomorrow another case will come along and we'll be fighting again."

Bruno nodded his agreement as he came around to sit down next to her. "Hey, Dana, you can't give up on us. I know it's not easy putting up with a bully like me, but we're great together."

"I think this relationship needs a lot of work."

"Okay, so we'll work on it. I can stop being a pig-headed bully and you can stop being..." He stopped, not sure if he should finish his sentence.

"Go on," she prompted. "I can stop being what?"

"Clara Kent, woman of steel." He paused to see if she was going to try to shove him again. "Well, maybe not completely," he conceded. "Maybe you could just get rid of the red-and-blue outfit."

"I'm not ditching the outfit. It cost two hundred dollars."

"And you look super in it."

Dana burst out laughing. Bruno took that as sign of encouragement and put his arms around her.

They sealed their agreement with a kiss. Dana hoped it was a truce that would last for a while, at least until her arm healed.

* * * * *